HOLD 'EM BACK!

By a ruse, Corsario, murderous leader of the Comanchero hordes of South Texas, had diverted the 8th Cavalry far north of its base. Left behind to fight off the raiders were three NCOs, six insubordinate troopers, the officers' wives and children, an old army scout and two Texas-born troubleshooters. Again and again the enemy attacked. Again and again the defenders fought back — fought on to the violent finish.

GAO

MARSHALL GROVER

HOLD 'EM BACK!

A Larry & Stretch Western

Complete and Unabridged

LINFORD
Leicester

First published in Great Britain in 1990 by
Horwitz Grahame Pty Limited
Australia

First Linford Edition
published 1996
by arrangement with
Horwitz Publications Pty Limited
Australia

British Library CIP Data

Grover, Marshall
    Larry & Stretch: hold 'em back!.
    —Large print ed.—
    Linford western library
    I. Title II. Series
    823 [F]

    ISBN 0–7089–7819–3

Published by
F. A. Thorpe (Publishing) Ltd.
Anstey, Leicestershire

Set by Words & Graphics Ltd.
Anstey, Leicestershire
Printed and bound in Great Britain by
T. J. Press (Padstow) Ltd., Padstow, Cornwall

This book is printed on acid-free paper

This one's for Lorraine Barfoot
A Lady of the Lone Star State
Marshall Grover
February, 1990

1

Happy Homecoming

BACK in Texas.

It felt good to Larry Valentine and Stretch Emerson until they encountered Jebediah Penn, an ex-army scout. They had drifted into the southernmost reaches of their homestate after quitting New Mexico with the intention of then making their way north to visit the scenes of their boyhood, maybe look up kinfolk and old friends.

"Flat and dusty," Larry observed a few moments before they sighted the other horseman. "But it's Texas, ol' buddy, so how does it feel?"

The taller drifter was a gangling beanpole six and a half feet tall, topping his brawny partner's generous height by a full three inches. He was

1

as blond as Larry was dark, as homely as Larry was ruggedly handsome and packed a second Colt at his left hip, being ambidextrous with hand-guns. He surveyed the arid terrain, heaved a sentimental sigh and declared, "Feels great to be back. We've been too long gone, runt."

All too true. Since wandering out of Texas after Appomattox, these trouble-prone nomads had seen a lot of country and a lot of action, locking horns with the scum of the frontier despite their craving for peace. The Northern Army had been their enemy during their service with the Confederate Cavalry. Since then, they had done battle with worse enemies, a more treacherous kind, the lawless as represented by bank bandits, horse thieves, cattle rustlers, stagecoach robbers, homicidal gunmen and every variety of human predator infesting the area as far north as the Canadian border, as far south as the Rio Grande, as far east as the winding Missouri and clear to the west coast. Back in their homestate for the first time since they couldn't remember when, they hoped with renewed fervor for a period of tranquillity and inactivity; the heroes were weary of conflict and the reputation they had built, thanks to the enthusiasm of the frontier Press.

Through the heat haze, they saw the lone rider. No mirage. He was real and headed their way and, though he kept his mount to an even pace, not hustling it, they sensed his urgency. He had seen them, was waving to them and sometimes glancing over his shoulder; he was approaching from the southeast.

"Damn," scowled Larry.

"Uh huh," grunted Stretch. "He's got trouble. We're lookin' to take it easy in Texas and the first hombre we see, he's got trouble."

They reined up, Larry delved into a saddlebag for his field glasses, the better to size up the oncoming wayfarer. Getting him into close focus, he remarked to his partner, "He's no spring chicken."

"Old timer?" prodded Stretch.

"And you're right about him," muttered Larry, lowering his glasses. "He's plenty fazed."

As he drew closer, the loner studied the tall horsemen, noting their weapons. Larry's sorrel and Stretch's pinto were equipped with saddle scabbards from which the butts of Winchesters jutted. The long guns and three revolvers added up to formidable fire power if their owners savvied how to use them, and he figured they did; they had the look of hard-boiled veterans.

Joining them, he observed, "Your critters look fresh enough, but mine could use spellin'." He dismounted, ground-reined his animal and, while fishing out tobacco pouch and corncob pipe, darted another glance to the southeast. "Oughta be time enough. I calculate I'm a far piece from where I spied on 'em." They swung down to hunker beside him, rolling cigarettes while he filled and lit his pipe. "Name's Jebediah Penn. Call me Jeb. Used to scout for the army. Durned if they didn't pasture me out. Too old — me? Hell, I dunno how old I am, but I'm still plenty spry."

They identified themselves while looking him over. Guessing his age might take time; his demeanor suggested there wouldn't be time enough. His hair was thick and grey and shoulder-length under a sweat-stained slouch hat. As much of his face as was visible through the whiskers was weatherbeaten, but his eyes were clear. Physically, he was small. But wiry, not an ounce of excess fat on him.

He repeated their names and, as had hundreds before him, declared he was sure he'd heard them of before.

"We'd as soon you hadn't, if it was up to us," grouched Larry. "A reputation — who needs it?"

"Well, you bucks bein' Texan like me, you know what a kill-crazy bastard he is, that Corsario."

"Jeb, we've been away from Texas many a long year," drawled Stretch. "Sorry. We never heard of him."

"Corsario's Spanish for Raider," frowned Larry. "He's some kind of boss-bandido?"

"Worse'n that," scowled Jeb. "Half-Comanche, half-Mex, and he heads up a whole band of Comancheros that's been raisin' hell north and south of the river. Real bad bunch, Injuns, Mexicanos and renegade whites — border trash."

When he sighted the big camp yesterday afternoon, the ex-scout had abandoned his plan to wander down to Monterey and stay idle a while. He hadn't ventured close enough to be detected. From good cover, he had studied the massed force through his spyglass. Corsario he easily identified, after which he had counted better than two hundred Comancheros. Plainly, Corsario was setting up a big coup which could mean grief and bloodshed for many border communities. Or worse.

"Worse?" challenged Larry.

"What if he was camped there waitin' for others to join him?" fretted Jeb. "Damn it, this wouldn't be the first time he's attacked an army post. And the headquarters of Colonel Delmer's Eighth Cavalry, the regiment I used to scout for, is northwest from here, Fort Mitchum. That's where I'm headed. The colonel's gotta be warned, and you boys're gonna ride along with me."

"You ain't askin' us, you're tellin' us," observed Stretch.

"On accounta you're Texans and most every horse soldier in the regiment's Texan or some other kinda Southerner," Jeb said vehemently. "Them and their womenfolk and a couple dozen kids. Whole families live at the fort."

"Families of officers and NCOs," reflected Larry. "That's the way of it, sure. Where a regiment's based, that's home."

"Three of us gotta better chance of

makin' it," Jeb pointed out. "If we ran into Comanchero scouts and I took an arrow, if one of you got unlucky too, there'd still be hope the third man could outrun 'em. So far, I'm the only one knew Corsario's rallyin' a raidin' party, a big'un. Now there's three of us know. But the Eighth dunno yet, and they gotta be told pronto, you savvy?"

"No argument, amigo," said Larry. "Point us to Fort Mitchum and we'll get movin' soon as your horse catches his wind." He glanced at his partner and ruefully remarked, "And we hoped things'd be quiet and peaceful back in Texas."

"We hope too much," shrugged Stretch. "We ought to give up on hopin' — forever."

"No matter how big a bunch Corsario's musterin', the soldier-boys at Mitchum can hold 'em off, but only if they get fair warnin'," muttered the old scout.

"Right," agreed Larry. "Otherwise

it'll be a surprise attack."

"And, like you always say, runt," Stretch reminded him. "Them that springs a surprise got 'emselves an edge."

The drifters smoked their quirleys down to one-inch stubs. Larry took a bottle from his saddlebag. All three men drank stiff shots and decided they were ready for anything. Jeb's animal was feeling lively again. They remounted and, with Jeb leading, started northwest. It was 9.45 a.m. and the temperature still rising; the expatriates had returned to their home-state at the hottest time of the year.

They rode four miles with their eyes alert and their rifles unsheathed. Jeb Penn's handgun was a Colt .44 with a seven and a half inch barrel, the cavalry model.

"Plenty water at the fort?" Larry asked.

"Three wells that's never yet dried up," said Jeb. "Plenty of everything at

Mitchum. I ain't sayin' it's like a town, but it's a . . . "

He paused to search his mind for the appropriate word. Larry supplied it.

"Community?"

"Yup, that's what it is," said Jeb. "The kids get their schoolin' and every soul eats regular. Big place, the fort, and every necessary's right inside them high stockades. There's chicken runs, a place for pigs, vegetable plots and root cellars and a corral fulla beef on the hoof."

"Catwalks for defendin' the parapets if needs be," guessed Stretch. "High you called it, that stockade fence."

"Safe place to hole up," Jeb assured them. "But, if trouble's comin', it's better they're ready for it. I figure we'll get there around — what time you got?"

Larry checked his watch.

"Twenty after ten."

"Nooncampin' could cost us an hour," opined Jeb. "Better we don't stop till we make the fort. I'd reckon we'll see it," he scanned the surrounding terrain, getting his bearings, "about five more hours."

During the hours of steady riding, during pauses to spell the horses, they maintained their vigilance. Not another soul to be seen on this sunbaked plain, as they drew closer to their destination, no sign of life in the stands of timber away north, no smoke rising above the tree tops.

By 2 p.m., the timber was lost from view and Fort Mitchum visible in the distance. Again Larry used his binoculars. The gateway, the only entrance to the fort, seemed massive, even taller than the stockades. He glimpsed two blue-uniformed cavalrymen following their approach from their vantage-point atop the near wall. Jeb read his mind and mumbled, "Won't be no challenge. They'll open up for us. Any trooper of that outfit'd know me a mile off."

He was impatient, so they coaxed their animals to a last burst of speed. Responding to his ragged yell, recognizing the voice and the man, one of the guards called an order. The other guard disappeared and, by the time they were finishing their advance, the great gates were opening.

Larry's disquiet began when they rode into Fort Mitchum and the gates were closed behind them. He reined up to scan the compound, the parade ground, the stockades with wooden steps leading up to the catwalks along all four walls, the roofs of the administration building, barracks, stables and other structures, some tiled, some shingled, adobe and clapboard and log the main building materials. He could hear childish voices; the small fry were reciting their multiplication tables. He saw several women appear on the porch of the headquarters building and others emerge from officers' and NCOs' quarters, their curiosity aroused by the arrival of the old scout and two tough-looking civilians in range clothes. Something was missing here.

A lot was missing. Stable doors were open and the only uniformed men he could see were the two gate guards and another lounging on the north catwalk.

Jeb Penn's disquiet was even greater. He bellowed to the barrel-chested sergeant descending from the south parapet.

"Mulligan! For pity's sakes — where is everybody?"

The NCO joined them as they dismounted. Before answering Jeb's shocked question, he eyed the strangers warily; the strangers identified themselves. He nodded, no longer wary.

"Yeah. Heard of you."

"He's Sergeant Emmett Mulligan," Jeb said impatiently. "Mulligan, what's happened here?"

"Most of the regiment's northbound for Rowansburg," said Mulligan. "Left day before yesterday. Deputy sheriff from Rowansburg, feller name of Gillis, near busted his horse's gut gettin' here. The Comancheros, Corsario's raiders,

13

are massin' up there. If you've been to Rowansburg, you'll recall it's dead centre of a big basin. Well, with Corsario's bunch ringin' the basin, it figures they mean to mount a big raid. Them towners'll fort up and do the best they can, but no chance they'll survive without the cavalry, so . . . "

"So — hell's sakes — how many troopers left here in the fort?" demanded Jeb.

"Just a handful." Mulligan stood arms akimbo and stared around. "That's Trooper Ainsworth patrollin' the north wall. Colonel wasn't about to take *him* along. Damn fool boy was catnappin' while on guard duty. Wasn't for Surgeon Major Richards puttin' in a plea for leniency, the colonel would've court-martialled him. Farrier Sergeant Ulric's guardin' the gate now and Quartermaster Sergeant Elvey helps out too. We got a half-dozen rowdies locked in the guardhouse sleepin' off a big booze spree. Damn jackasses been cookin' their own corn liquor."

"Who's in charge — the colonel wouldn't take every officer with him," Jeb said urgently.

"Colonel decided one officer's all he could spare," said the sergeant. "They drew straws and Captain Blore drew the short one. You could say he's in command till the regiment gets back from whippin' the Comancheros at Rowansburg, but . . . "

"What d'you mean — I could say?" scowled Jeb.

"He's confined to his quarters, laid up," said Mulligan. He winced. Jeb's dismay and the drifters' grim expressions were getting to him. "Took a fall comin' down from a catwalk yesterday mornin', broke a leg and cracked a couple ribs."

"Aw, hell!" gasped Jeb.

"You ever gonna tell me what you . . . ?" began Mulligan.

"Jeb'll only have to say it the once if you're with us when he reports to the officer in charge," said Larry.

15

"Sounds reasonable," frowned Mulligan. "I'll take you to him."

The spent horses were, for the time being, left tied in the shade by the officers' quarters. Mulligan led the bad news carriers into the building and along a corridor to rap at a door. It was opened by a woman in her late thirties wearing a strictly utilitarian gown and a troubled expression.

"The captain is resting, Sergeant," she murmured. "Hallo, Mister Penn, what a surprise!"

"Mrs Blore, ma'am." Jeb and the trouble-shooters bared their heads. "Sorry about your man, but I gotta talk to him — right now — no time to waste."

Without another word, she admitted them. Propped up by pillows in the bed, the mustached, well-barbered and currently irascible Captain Tom Blore frowned at the sergeant, the old scout and the uncommonly tall strangers. Before he could voice a question, Jeb said his piece and without rambling.

Larry felt the warning should not be delivered with the woman present, but that was a brief thought; she was an army wife.

Blore's eyes widened.

"Jeb — you're certain?" he challenged.

"Told you I recognized the son of a — beggin' your pardon, ma'am," mumbled Jeb.

"At ease, Mister Penn," sighed Marj Blore, sinking into a chair. "That's no doubt what Corsario is. And all Comancheros."

"Lord Almighty!" breathed Blore. "That deputy from Rowansburg — convinced everybody . . . !"

"Including Colonel Delmer himself," his wife reminded him.

"Arrived on a lathered horse," muttered Blore. "The man was exhausted we thought. He waited only long enough to report the situation up north — which we now know to be a lie — then started back again on a fresh horse and with supplies for his journey. I think he

17

refilled his canteen, but he didn't even linger for a meal. He said — he couldn't wait to get back to his wife and children." He eyed Larry expectantly. "I sense you have something to say, Mister Valentine. I'm familiar with your reputation. Well?"

"This Gillis hombre, even if he wore a badge . . . " began Larry.

"He did," interjected Mulligan.

" . . . he's no lawman," Larry continued. "The tin star was genuine enough — likely snatched off of a real deputy while the Comancheros were raidin' some border settlement. We got to believe he was Corsario's own courier. His job was to near empty Fort Mitchum, and he did it good." He nodded to the captain's wife. "Sorry, ma'am, but it's plain enough Corsario'll mount a raid."

"He ain't up north," Jeb said bluntly. "He's southeast. I'm guessin' what Larry's thinkin' and — he's right. It ain't Rowansburg that's gonna be attacked. It's this fort."

"Which is almost defenceless," said Marj Blore; the drifters marvelled at her fatalism. If she felt fear, she didn't show it. "Tom?"

Blore was scowling at his splinted leg.

"I have to go along with Jeb's reasoning and Mister Valentine's. But what can Corsario hope to gain . . . ?" He broke off, eyeing Jeb again. "You have a theory about that?"

"Nobody's gonna take no comfort from what I'm sayin', but I savvy Comancheros, so I gotta say it," growled Jeb. "This skunk Corsario, he's got big ideas, hankers to raid and loot farther into Texas and all along the border. So he needs a lotta horses and weapons, plenty ammunition. The more scum he recruits, the more he needs of everything."

He hesitated.

"Don't stop now," frowned Blore.

"Hostages — women and kids," muttered Jeb.

"Yeah," Stretch grimaced in disgust. "Big coup. He wouldn't have to grab many."

"Not every woman and kid here, just a few'd be enough," nodded Larry. "The regiment comes back, finds them that stayed behind — dead and wounded — and some officers' wives, some kids missin'."

"Corsario'll leave the livin' to pass on his demands," said Jeb. "The Eighth turns over its horses to him, every gun, every round of ammunition. Straight trade. Everything he wants . . . "

"In return for the hostages," breathed Blore.

"I'm with Jeb," said Larry. "That's his plan — so we're just gonna have to disappoint him."

"By holding out until the regiment returns to disperse the raiding parties, offering stiff resistance with all the firepower we can muster," decided Blore. "Of course the regiment will return. When the colonel reaches Rowansburg and learns we've been duped, he'll start south again." Grim-eyed, he added, "Meanwhile, Fort Mitchum will be under siege."

"You gents know the territory 'tween here and Rowansburg — my partner and me've been away too long," said Larry. "Any chance one of us could head off the regiment this side of Rowansburg and turn 'em back?"

"If I thought you could do that, you'd be headed north on a fresh horse by now." Jeb shook his head. "No, it wouldn't help none. Ain't likely you'd sight 'em till you sighted Rowansburg too. They rode out day before yesterday don't forget."

"As civilians, you gentlemen are under no obligation to the Eighth Cavalry," Blore reminded the tall men. "It's your right to disassociate yourselves from the problem here. You could leave as soon as your horses are rested and fed." They eyed him blankly; he managed a wry grin. "Sorry. As officer in charge, it's my duty to say that."

"So you said it, and no offence," shrugged Stretch.

"But we ain't leavin', Captain," said Larry.

"Thank you," said Blore. "Your aid in defending Fort Mitchum will be much appreciated. Sergeant Mulligan, jog my memory. Our strength?"

"Weapons and ammunition aplenty, sir," said Mulligan. "Those booze-hounds in the guard-house, six of 'em, got to be sober by now. I don't know about the Ainsworth kid . . . "

"Trooper Martin Ainsworth's post should be the infirmary," Blore insisted. "I know he's unpopular with the other soldiers and I'm not forgetting he was found sleeping on guard duty."

"There was a reason," offered his wife. "Up till he began walking guard, he'd been studying the medical books the surgeon major loaned him — for hours."

"He has to be regarded as an amateur medical orderly, but he's efficient, by Godfrey," declared Blore. "After my stupid accident — let's not forget this, Sergeant — it was young Ainsworth who taped my ribs and set and splinted my leg, and Major Richards couldn't have done better. He'll be invaluable in the infirmary."

"Well, comes to patchin' wounds or diggin' out bullets, he's all we got," Mulligan conceded. "So, for mannin' the parapets, there'll be Trooper Yarrow and his hard case buddies, three sergeants, meanin' Elvey, Ulric and me, Jeb and . . . " He glanced at Larry and Stretch, "our fiddlefoot friends here, who've fought every kind of frontier scum, includin' Comancheros, for — it'd be near twenty years, right?"

"About that long," Stretch said casually.

"You're my second in command as of right now, Sergeant," said Blore. "Naturally I'll do my share of . . . "

"Tom, you can't!" pleaded his wife.

"I have a crutch," he said firmly. "I won't be a hundred percent mobile and may have difficulty using a rifle but, if the worst happens, if the enemy forces entry, I'll have my pistol and sabre. No arguments, my dear, if you please."

"The other ladies have to be told," said Larry. "And the kids ought to be kept together."

"Inform the colonel's lady of the situation," Blore urged his wife. "A barracks could be converted to a dormitory for the children."

Rising, Marj offered an assurance to the trouble-shooters.

"Don't be worrying about the women of Port Mitchum, gentlemen. There'll be no screaming nor swooning. Bear in mind we are cavalry wives."

"Jeb, would you accompany Mrs Blore?" the captain requested. "They know you well and respect you, Mrs Delmer and the other ladies. And, as a morale-booster, you could take Mister Valentine and his friend along." He didn't fail to note the drifters' quick exchange of glances. "Humor me," he begged. "I know you resent the notoriety forced on you by the Press, but the ladies, most of them, will have heard of you. I'm sure your presence will reassure them. Fort Mitchum can use a couple of living legends in this time of crisis, to put it mildly."

"Whatever you say, Captain," shrugged Larry.

As the drifters began following Jeb and Marj out, Blore told Mulligan, "You'd best apprise Sergeants Elvey and Ulric of the situation and have them mount guard. It may be some time before the raiding party appears . . . "

"That's Jeb's hunch, sir," nodded Mulligan.

"But they'd best keep a sharp lookout," said Blore. "Talk to young Ainsworth too. It's vital he understands what'll be expected of him."

The colonel's lady, Mattie Delmer, was socializing with other women on the broad porch of the administration block when Marj and the three civilians approached. Larry noted two of Mrs Delmer's companions were young. He figured the dark-haired, hazel-eyed beauty to be barely twenty-one and the slim, slightly freckled blonde girl to be still in her teens. They climbed to the porch and Marj performed introductions. The dark-haired beauty proved to be Sarah, daughter of the Delmers, the teenager Naomi, daughter of Major Ira Landis and his wife, Elmira, also present. The drifters were trading appraisals with as dignified a group of women as they would ever encounter.

Jeb was accorded a warm welcome, the gracefully aging Mattie Delmer good-humoredly remarking, "I protested the colonel's decision, Jeb, told him you're too active for retirement whatever your age. And here you are, looking as agile as ever — if a little sombre."

"The famous Lone Star Trouble-Shooters, favorites of the Fourth Estate," her daughter dryly observed; the tall men sensed scepticism, but stayed impassive, showing no resentment. "Surely such gallant knights-errant should be in uniform or serving as Federal law officers. I believe your penchant for brawling has landed you in innumerable town jails, which does seem a waste of time and your considerable talents — if we're to believe all we read in the newspapers."

"Larry and Stretch — oh, my!" Naomi Landis giggled excitedly.

"Serious news, Mattie," said Marj.

She relayed the information delivered by the old scout while the trouble-shooters studied reactions. Fort Mitchum's commandant had been deceived by a fake lawman, obviously a Comanchero. The 8th Cavalry was far from its base and at the mercy of the dreaded Corsario and all his followers until the regiment turned back from Rowansburg and returned to base. Meanwhile, the fort would undoubtedly be attacked.

"Won't happen rightaway," Jeb pointed out. "Main bunch was a long ways southeast when I spied on 'em. So we got time to — uh — get set."

He had no option but to offer his opinion bluntly; he knew no other way. Again, the drifters studied reactions, this time to the old scout's warning as to Corsario's strategy, the acquisition of as many mounts and weapons as he demanded in exchange for the hostages he intended taking. The women were alarmed — why wouldn't they be? But there were no shocked gasps, no tears, no hysterical outbursts; these were ladies of the US Cavalry.

"So there is much to be done," Mattie Delmer said briskly. "We have to get busy, ladies."

Beth Richards, wife of the regiment's medical officer, remarked, "Petticoats to be sacrificed, my dears. I'll have Trooper Ainsworth check our supply of bandaging and dressings, but I fear George packed most of it for the advance on Rowansburg — where there'll be no fighting at all."

"Trooper Ainsworth — too squeamish for combat anyway," Sarah said disdainfully. "I'm sure he'll feel safe in the infirmary."

"Food," said the colonel's wife. "We'd best get to cooking. Quartermaster Sergeant Elvey will be too busy breaking out weapons and ammunition to bother himself with preparing meals. There are not only the children to be fed. The men manning the parapets have to keep up their strength."

"I can use a rifle — and with considerable skill." Sarah aimed this brag at the tall men, challengingly. "Army women aren't ignorant in the use of weapons."

Larry finally addressed her.

"I can't speak for Sergeant Mulligan, just for my partner and me," he growled. "And we don't want to see any women on them catwalks, not totin' guns anyway." He redonned his Stetson. "If you ladies'll excuse us, we got to get busy too."

He moved away from the administration block with Stretch and Jeb, the latter confiding, as if they cared a damn, "That high-falutin' Miss Sarah's spoke for. Way I hear it, she'll be hitchin' up with one of her pa's officers purty soon, Lieutenant Grescoe."

"Hooray for the lieutenant," Stretch said with a grimace. "And he's welcome."

The bulky Farrier Sergeant Jake Ulric and the just as hefty Quartermaster Sergeant Moses Elvey were busy, the blacksmith on guard on the cat-walk left of the gateway, Elvey toting rifles and boxes of ammunition from the armory. Mulligan was striding toward the guardhouse, so Jeb and the Texans tagged along.

When Mulligan unlocked and opened the door and ordered the unruly six out, they emerged slowly, blinking against the sunlight, swearing a lot, but sober, no longer hungover. The 8th Cavalry's most consistent insubordinates were as scruffy a half-dozen as could be found in any regiment, hardheads, uniforms grubby, dispositions ugly.

"Line up, stand to attention and listen careful!" barked Mulligan.

As they formed a ragged line, a burly redhead retorted, "The hell with you, Mulligan."

"Shuddup, Trooper Gleddon," growled Mulligan. "Till I'm through talkin', use your ears, not that big mouth of yours." For the benefit of the three civilians, he named the other hard cases. "Troopers Yarrow, Sykes, O'Curran, Janney and Frost — listen up!" Tersely, he then reported the scout's sighting of a heavy force of Comancheros to the southeast, far from where the 8th Cavalry expected to find them, thanks to the false news delivered by a bogus lawman. "That clear enough for you knuckleheads? Those damn Comancheros mean to raid Fort Mitchum and steal women and kids for hostages — but we're gonna hold out against 'em for as long as it takes the regiment to come on back and send 'em runnin'."

"Oughta be quite a party," commented the long-jawed Pike Yarrow. "More of 'em than us."

"Helluva lot more," complained scrawny Jerry Sykes.

"We're gonna be outnumbered, and then some," grouched flat-nosed Biff Janney.

"The divil with 'em," shrugged florid Dan O'Curran. "We're gonna have to shoot faster and straighter'n them stinkin' heathen scum."

"Ain't nothin' else we can do is what it gets down to," shrugged the almost totally bald Curly Frost.

"Captain Blore's in command, but he's laid up, so you'll take orders mostly from me," said Mulligan.

"What d'you mean — mostly?" demanded Gleddon.

"If my Irish luck runs out, you'd better heed these boys," said Mulligan, indicating the trouble-shooters. "Guess you've heard of Valentine and Emerson. Used to be Confederate troopers. Comes to fightin', they're a couple pros from way back."

Gleddon, it seemed, had been born some hundreds of miles north of the Mason-Dixon line. It was also evident he had scant respect for the legendary outlaw-fighters. He bunched his fists, uttered an aspersion on the mating habits of the trouble-shooters' forebears and truculently announced, "It'll be a cold day in hell when I take orders from a no-account reb!" He broke from the line and, to Larry's irritation, ignored Mulligan's reprimand and advanced on him threateningly. "So you're Valentine?"

"Easy now, Red," cautioned Larry.

"You don't look so all-fired tough to me," scowled the big redhead. "I'm a better man than you are — and I'm gonna prove it here and now!"

His cronies guffawed and urged him on; Mulligan's protests fell on deaf ears and, for the first time that he could recall, Larry was mentally rehearsing his retaliation. Every able-bodied man of Fort Mitchum was needed — desperately. That included this bumptious roughneck bent on beating his brains out. He would have to subdue Gleddon, but couldn't afford to disable him.

When he dodged Gleddon's wild swing, he could have struck back hard enough to fracture the red-head's jaw, break his nose or dent a rib. Instead, he landed a roundhouse right that bounced off the side of Gleddon's head, spun him and sent him pitching to the dust.

How seriously had he injured a much-needed soldier?

"On your feet, Gleddon!" fumed Mulligan.

2

Prelude to Battle

GLEDDON spat grit, rolled over and lurched upright, glaring at Larry.

"You outa your damn mind, Trooper?" raged Jeb. "There's gonna be a bloody war here! We gotta make ready to fight off raiders! You pick a helluva time for tanglin' with a feller that's on *our side*!"

"Consarn you, Gleddon, if you step outa line one more time, you'll be on report!" warned Mulligan. "I'll see you court-martialled when the regiment gets back!"

"Red, this ain't no time for quarrellin' amongst ourselves," chided Stretch. "If you're hot for a fight, save it for when them border killers come a'raidin'."

"Good advice, Red," frowned Larry.

"I owe you — damn you!" snarled Gleddon, pointing to him. "For us, it don't end here, Valentine! When this trouble's over, we're gonna finish this — if you can work up the nerve!"

"If you got your mind set on it, that's how it'll be," shrugged Larry.

"I can beat the tar outa you and I aim to prove it!" declared Gleddon. "I *gotta* prove it!"

"Fine," nodded Larry. "Meantime, let's get ready to fight Comancheros."

"The women'll be cookin'," said Mulligan. "Troopers Sykes, Frost and Yarrow eat first. Troopers Gleddon, O'Curran and Frost, draw arms and ammunition and man the parapets till you're relieved. Move your asses!"

As the troopers dispersed, Larry asked, "Which stable for our horses, Sarge?"

"Any stalls in any stable — help yourselves," Mulligan offered, hurrying away.

"You boys mind tendin' my critter too?" begged Jeb. "I hanker to get up by the gate with my spyglass."

"Sure, Jeb," said Larry. "We'll see you later."

While they were leading their mounts and the scout's to a stable for feeding, watering and bedding down, Stretch sighed resignedly.

"Look at us peace-lovin' travellers," he drawled.

"Think of why we headed back to Texas. Too much action elsewhere we said. Home in Texas with our own kind, we'll get to take it easy we said, look up old friends and talk of old times we said. And what're we doin' now?"

"Just like always, beanpole," shrugged Larry. "Gettin' ready for a fight, a big'un, because there ain't nothin' else we *can* do."

"I *know* what we're doin'," grouched Stretch.

"So why'd you ask?" challenged Larry.

"Seemed like a fair question," Stretch said helplessly. "Even though I knew the damn answer."

Marj Blore became agitated the moment she rejoined her husband. He was out of bed and practising, trying to familiarize himself with something he had never needed before, a crutch. Back and forth he stumped in his nightshirt and slippers, sweat beading on his brow.

"Tom, don't do that!" she pleaded. "Be reasonable!"

"*You* be reasonable," he retorted as she confronted him. "Confound it, Marj, are you afraid these damn injuries have affected my brain? I'm thinking clearly, thinking of my responsibilities. I'm in command here and a crisis has arisen and I have to deal with it. *Duty*, Marj."

"Colonel Delmer wouldn't expect you to . . . " she began.

"He didn't anticipate I'd fall and break a leg," he pointed out. "It was an accident nobody expected, especially me. Had he left Ira Landis in charge, Waldo Toone or Mat Grescoe, had any of them suffered the same damn mishap, what do you suppose they'd be doing under these circumstances? Exactly as I'm doing. The officer in charge, having been warned of an attack, has to do the best he can possibly do."

"Forgive me," she sighed. "It's just — oh my darling, if you could see yourself. This is pitiful."

For her benefit, he grinned encouragingly and kissed her.

"As I recall — going back quite a few years — you had two choices," he said. "Another suitor, my rival, of whom your father warmly approved. Quite the dandy, wasn't he? Chief cashier in his father's bank. By now, he's probably manager of that bank. What was his name again?"

"Rodney — Roger — something like that," she said. "I haven't thought of him in years."

"You chose a shavetail lieutenant of the US Cavalry and what he had to offer," he muttered. "Not enough, Marj?"

"More than enough," she whispered.

"You became an army wife," he said gently. "And a damn fine one. You have as much courage, as much strength of will as Mattie Delmer herself. Don't change now, my dear. Not at a time like this."

"I won't change," she promised. "But what do you want from me, Tom Blore? Indifference? An army wife I may be, but you *are* injured and I'm still a woman and human. Wouldn't Mattie and her lovely daughter fret if the colonel suffered such a mishap?"

"I guess so," he said. "But don't overdo the fretting and fussing — please?" A discreet rapping at the door. He frowned over his wife's shoulder. "Who?"

"Trooper Ainsworth, sir," was the reply. "Permission to re-check your splints?"

"You may come in, Trooper," he called, and Marj moved away from him.

Martin Ainsworth, though in uniform, would never, *could* never, look like a typical cavalryman. He was passably handsome but reticent, sensitive-featured, his hair cut short, his brown eyes solemn. Standing a shade under five feet ten inches, he was lean of build, deft of movement and, as Blore had observed, an excellent horseman. In demeanor, however, he was decidedly unmilitary.

"Mrs Blore." He nodded respectfully. "My apologies for the intrusion, sir." Then he frowned. "You're not resting, sir."

"Have you been alerted to the current situation?" demanded Blore.

"The possibility of a Comanchero raid, yes, sir," said Ainsworth.

"The probability," Blore corrected. "So I've no choice but to test my mobility with this infernal crutch."

"That may not be too premature, may even be beneficial," said Ainsworth. He moved close and dropped to one knee. "With your permission, sir." Lifting the patient's nightshirt, he carefully inspected the splinted leg.

41

"Satisfactory, I think. Yes, the splints haven't loosened. Do you mind moving a few paces so that I may observe?"

Blore did that and, for a while, they appeared incongruous to Marj, her husband working himself along with the aid of the crutch, Ainsworth keeping pace on all fours, still with the nightshirt raised and his intent gaze on the splinted leg.

"Satisfied?" challenged Blore.

"Everything staying in place, sir," said Ainsworth, getting to his feet. "But, with respect, I advise extreme care, no attempt at swift movement . . . "

"You're starting to sound like your idol," Blore remarked.

"My idol, sir?" blinked Ainsworth.

"Surgeon Major Richards," said Ainsworth. "Admit it, boy."

"Begging the captain's pardon, I don't idolize the major," Ainsworth assured him. "But I very much admire his surgical skill and I'll always appreciate his permitting me to assist him, to learn so much."

"We have ample proof of your ability to treat broken limbs and dented ribs," Blore conceded. "But could you find the courage to, for instance, probe for and extract a bullet?"

"I believe so, sir," said Ainsworth. "You'll recall Corporal Carmody's injury some eleven months ago, a revolver accidentally discharging, the bullet lodging in his left side?"

"Corporal Carmody is quite fit now," nodded Blore. "I wish he were here instead of with the regiment on a wild goose chase to Rowansburg. He's an excellent marksman."

"Major Richards allowed me to observe the operation, insisted I watch his every movement and was kind enough to explain the procedure," said Ainsworth. "I'm sure, should it be necessary, I could extract a bullet. Even if it were a chest wound, I'd feel compelled to make the effort. And, yes, I'd have the nerve for it."

"Very well, Trooper Ainsworth, we may soon find urgent need for whatever skill you've gained from being Major Richard's volunteer assistant," said Blore. "So heed Sergeant Mulligan's orders. When the raid begins, confine yourself to the infirmary. As a casualty, you'd be of no use to your comrades."

"Yes, sir, I'll remember that," Ainsworth promised.

"Dismissed," said Blore.

"Sir."

Ainsworth saluted him and quietly withdrew. When the door closed and her husband returned to the bed to perch on its edge, Marj Blore shook her head sadly and murmured, "That poor, sensitive young man — there *is* somebody he idolizes."

"Does he confide in you?" he asked incredulously.

"He'd never do that," she said with a wistful smile. "You've seen how discreet he is, how reticent."

"Then how would you know . . . ?"

"Observation, and woman's intuition."

"Who?"

"Just between us, Tom."

"As you wish. At any other time, I wouldn't be in the least curious about a lovelorn trooper but Ainsworth and whatever he learned from George Richards are vital to our defence. If we suffer casualties, that young feller has to concentrate all his efforts . . . "

"I'm sure his personal feelings won't affect his work. He's really dedicated."

"So? Which of you women is he mooning over? Beth Richards? Leona Harrington — *you*?"

"It's Sarah," said Marj.

Blore grimaced in exasperation.

"Ridiculous. His commanding officer's daughter — and she betrothed to Lieutenant Grescoe? I hope you're mistaken."

"So do I," she said. "But I've seen the way he looks at her. She doesn't suspect of course — treats him with scorn. It's sad, don't you think?"

"Marj, it's *nothing*," he scowled. "It's trivial, compared to the crisis we have to deal with, fourteen men facing the prospect of holding off a horde of

Comancheros, three of them civilians, one trooper who can't be allowed join the fight — me, the officer in charge, restricted by a broken leg."

"Don't reproach yourself," she chided. "You weren't careless. Accidents do happen."

"Polly Glynn will have to forget about playing school-teacher," he muttered. "I want the children confined to a barracks when the raid begins, safest place for them."

"That's all being taken care of," she assured him. "We're converting Barracks Four to a dormitory. It's big enough, and we can separate the boys from the girls by running a line along the centre and hanging blankets. Try to relax, Tom. Until something happens, you should rest."

"Do you hear yourself, do you realize what you're saying?" he challenged. "Relax? Damn it, Marj, I'm in charge here! This is no time for you to coddle me!"

"Just promise me . . . " She pleaded

resignedly. "When it — all begins . . . "

"You don't have to say it," he said, taking her hand. "I'll take no foolish risks, but I do have to honor my responsibilities. You're an army wife. You of all people should understand. Duty first, Marj."

"I understand," she nodded. "All too well."

In the late afternoon, the trouble-shooters climbed to the south parapet to join the old scout. Jeb's spyglass was directed to the southeast. Elvey and Ulric were in position on the catwalk on the other side of the gates.

"Make a guess," urged Larry.

"Sometime tomorrow," opined Jeb. "To reach the fort in time to mount a night attack, they'd've had to travel fast in the heat of this day. Time they got here, their horses'd be draggin' their feet. They ain't about to come a'raidin' on winded horses."

"And you figured they were waitin' anyway," drawled Stretch. "Waitin' for more border scum to come join 'em."

47

"You could bet your butts on that," growled Jeb. "Got big ideas has Corsario. I savvy how the bastard thinks."

"How come you learned so much about him?" asked Larry.

"There was this rurale I palavered with a time back," confided Jeb. "Name of Santilla — Miguel Santilla. Him and some other rurales captured a renegade, skunk called Ortega. He'd been spotted ridin' with the Corsario bunch, so, when they nailed him in some Chihuahua settlement, they tried him muy pronto, stood him against a wall and shot him. The thing is, while they had him cooped, this Ortega bragged some about the boss-Comanchero. And that's why I know what kind of a hellion he is."

"Gettin' too big for his britches?" prodded Larry.

"Could be a little loco," scowled Jeb. "Maybe *more'n* a little."

"The crazy ones can be sly," muttered

Stretch. "They're the most dangerous, we've always found."

"Claims he'll be like a king," Jeb said scathingly.

"So he sure as hell's got big ideas," remarked Larry.

"With enough horses, enough trash sidin' him and with enough guns, he figures he'll rule all of southwest Texas," declared Jeb. "Whites'll have two choices. They call him boss or they're good for the buzzards — them and their women, after his scum're through with the women. Not the kids. They'll be kept alive. He'll raise 'em and train 'em to be Comancheros."

"How d'you like that for big ideas?" Stretch challenged Larry.

"If he can take hostages here, he'll be on the way to gettin' everything he wants," nodded Larry. With no hint of bravado, almost casually, he added, "Well, we can't let that happen, can we?"

"Nope," grunted Stretch. "Onliest thing we can do is hold him off till all them horse soldiers come a'hustlin' back to this here fort."

"You bucks thinkin' we're bitin' off more'n we can chaw?" challenged Jeb.

"We're thinkin' there ain't a damn thing we can do 'cept keep the raiders busy and down as many of 'em as we can draw a bead on," said Larry.

"Mose Elvey calculates we got guns aplenty, all the ammo we're gonna need too," offered Jeb.

They were now joined by Sergeant Mulligan who, after peering southeast a moment, said, "Chow in a little while. Eat up here if you want. The ladies'll fetch it."

"Obliged to the ladies, Emmett," nodded Jeb. "Reckon I'll stay put a couple more hours 'fore I catch some shuteye."

To the drifters, the sergeant muttered an assurance.

"Those hardnoses out of the guardhouse, don't be frettin' about 'em. When the chips're down, fightin' is what they do best."

"That's how I figured 'em," shrugged Larry.

"I meant what I told 'em, Valentine," said Mulligan. "It ain't regulation but, if my luck runs out, you're the one they'd better heed. My ol' buddies . . . " He gestured toward the other NCOs. "Good men, both of 'em, and same rank as me. Mose and Jake'll handle their share of the fightin' and they've had plenty target practice, but they don't savvy battle tactics, ain't supposed to. Mose savvies supplies, how to store and issue 'em. Jake's as smart a blacksmith as you'd find any place. It's just they ain't combat sergeants like me."

"Sure," said Larry.

"Meanwhile, if you got any ideas, I ain't too proud to listen," Mulligan offered. "We're gettin' organized pretty good. I've been plenty busy, busy enough to maybe forget somethin'. So?"

Larry turned to scan the big compound and the buildings beyond.

"Good water supply," he mused.

"Three wells — you've seen 'em," said Mulligan.

"Fire arrows," said Larry. "Corsario's half-Comanche and half or more of his bunch'd be full-bloods. That means, sooner or later, they might hit on the notion of shootin' fire arrows, do some burnin' here."

"The colonel'll call that diversion tactics," said Mulligan, grimacing. "Troopers can't fight fires and raiders at the same time."

"We can make it easier for any that need to douse a fire fast," opined Larry. "We don't wait till it happens. You detail a soldier to fill every bucket he can find, set 'em back of and both sides of every barracks, every place built more of timber than adobe, every place that'd start burnin' if a fire arrow hit it. That'll be one way we'll be sure the Eighth don't come hurryin' back to a burnt-out fort."

"One way you say?" prodded Mulligan. "There's another way?"

"Sure is," nodded Larry. "But it kind of depends."

"On what?" asked Mulligan.

"Night or day, a flyin' arrow's a fast-movin' target," Larry pointed out. "Good target for a rifleman — if he's a right smart sharpshooter. That what they are, Red and his buddies?"

"The cavalry most always fights movin' targets, friend," said Mulligan. "Gleddon and Yarrow and those other rowdies, yeah, they're smart shots."

"Best time to stop a fire arrow's when it's on its way," said Stretch. "If you aim good, a bullet'll do it every time."

"I'll pass that on to every man," Mulligan decided. "And young Ainsworth ain't busy in the infirmary — yet — so I'll have him set full buckets where they'll be handy when they're needed." Before leaving them, he appraised the tall men and said good-humoredly, but with obvious sincerity, "With you hot shots helpin' out, our chances of holdin' Corsario's raiders off are gettin' better. It's mighty fortunate you never turned outlaw. I'd sooner have you with us than agin us."

Entering the infirmary a few minutes later, he found Trooper Ainsworth checking the contents of cabinets containing medical supplies and surgical instruments. He gave the order for Ainsworth to take every pail from the quartermaster's store, fill them at the wells and distribute them as Larry had suggested. As was his way, he also explained the reason for this precaution. There was time, he assured himself. Soldiers were trained to obey without question but, in his experience, it was better for them to know why.

Ainsworth's reaction intrigued him.

"I'll see to it at once, Sergeant. It's not for me to say, but may I say it just the same? Great idea. It could save precious time."

"You know, kid, you got the makin's of a damn good soldier," frowned Mulligan.

"Thank you, Sergeant," Ainsworth

acknowledged. "But it was inexcusable, my falling asleep on guard duty, wasn't it? Almost as great a fault as dropping my weapon and fleeing from the enemy?"

"I could be wrong, but I don't reckon you'd do that," decided Mulligan. "All right, you got your orders. Get on with it."

Martin Ainsworth hurried away to begin his chore.

Sarah Delmer climbed the steps to the catwalk with Naomi Landis following, she carrying a laden plate in one hand, a cup of coffee in the other, Naomi balancing a tray containing two more of the same, plus a platter of sliced bread.

"Suppertime, Mister Penn," Sarah announced, as they moved to the three men left of the fort's entrance.

"'Obliged, Miss Sarah," Jeb mumbled, accepting his meal.

The tall men thanked Naomi and began eating.

"Mister Emerson must be terribly

hungry," she grinned.

"Nope, that's how he always eats," Larry assured her. "He claims I was born curious. Well, he was born hungry. Ten minutes after he's through eatin', he's hungry again. And you don't have to call him or me 'Mister', little lady. You bein' some younger'n Miss Sarah, you can call us Uncle Larry and . . ."

"Uncle Stretch?" chuckled the girl. "That sounds so funny."

Jeb swallowed a mouthful and said approvingly, "*That* sounds *good*, Miss Naomi, you laughin'."

"Right," agreed Larry. "Means you're bein' yourself and keepin' your nerve. Keep on doin' that, hear?"

"I'll try hard," she promised.

"When the raid begins, Mister Valentine, don't be distracted if I and other ladies join the fighting," said Sarah.

"You got a short memory, seems to me," frowned Larry, fork half-raised to mouth. "I already told you we

56

don't want to see no women on the catwalks."

"You aren't in charge here," she coolly retorted. "And may I remind you our lives — or worse — are at stake? Pardon my using the old cliche — a fate worse than death — but if Corsario wins, if he seizes women as hostages, do you seriously believe he'd return us unscathed? I'd rather die in the fighting than find myself at the mercy of those savages."

"I guess I savvy what it means — distracted," muttered Jeb.

"So do I," Larry told Sarah. "The thing is my partner and me couldn't help gettin' distracted."

"In a rough fix, we always try to protect women," explained Stretch. "Old habit, you know? And we can't shake it."

"So heroic, so chivalrous." Sarah smiled, and Larry didn't admire the way she smiled, the derision. "But, unless I'm mistaken, you're really misogynists."

Stretch's jaw fell.

"We're — *what* . . . ?"

"Oh, do forgive me," she begged, but boredly. "How remiss of me to forget the famous legends had very little education."

The eager to help Naomi murmured, "A misogynist is a woman hater — and I don't think that's what you are."

"Well, Holy Hannah, we don't hate females, do we, runt?" protested Stretch. Larry was eating; he shook his head. "Shucks, no. It's just — uh — they can be a nuisance sometimes, right?"

Larry munched, swallowed and said, "Right."

"The ever-overbearing male," Sarah said scornfully, drawing closer to Stretch. Her next move took both drifters by surprise. It was done swiftly, deftly, her emptying Stretch's left-side holster, twirling the .45 by its trigger-guard, then hefting it, testing its weight. "Fine pistol, nice balance." She twirled it again and returned it to its holster.

"You see, Mister Valentine? Ladies of the cavalry aren't unfamiliar with firearms."

"Who taught you to spin a hogleg that way?" asked Larry.

"My fiance," she said. "Lieutenant Mathew Grescoe."

"That's real nice," said Larry. "Real smart trick. But a woman oughtn't try it with a full-loaded Colt. If the lieutenant didn't teach you that, he should've."

"I'm terrified," she said, daintily covering a yawn with a slim hand. "I've antagonized the famous Mister Valentine." She turned and moved toward the steps. "Coming, Naomi?"

"I think I'll wait and collect the dishes," decided Naomi.

"And ogle our brave protectors no doubt," drawled Sarah. "Very well, dear, if that's your idea of fun."

When she had descended to the compound and was out of earshot, the freckled blonde earnestly assured the tall men, "She was just amusing herself, not really being mean."

"Whatever you say, Miss Naomi," Larry replied as he resumed eating.

"I want to tell you all the ladies know your reputation," said Naomi. "And we're so grateful you're with us now." She smiled amiably. "It's true what I've read and heard. You do seem to show up where and when you're most needed."

"Not on purpose," grouched Larry.

"Just happens, Miss Naomi," shrugged Stretch. "It's our hex."

"Plum fortunate for Fort Mitchum, honey," said Jeb. The familiarity was excusable; he had known the daughter of Ira and Elmira Landis since she was eighteen inches shorter and her hair in pigtails. "These bucks don't brag, but they're scrappers from way back. Fightin' kinda comes natural to 'em."

"What exciting times you've known," she said admiringly. "But how dangerous it must have been. You've suffered so much. I know you're — no strangers to pain. You've so often been wounded, almost killed."

Her deep concern for their welfare embarrassed Stretch, who could never cope with adulation. Not so embarrassed, more inclined to appreciate this girl's well-meant compassion, Larry made a prediction to himself. When of age, she would not have developed a mean streak; too bad he couldn't feel the same about the high and mighty Sarah Delmer.

"Real fine chow," remarked Jeb.

"Coffee's good too," approved Stretch.

"You spoken for too, Miss Naomi?" asked Larry.

"No." She smiled teasingly. "Why? Have I won your tough old bachelor heart?"

"Just askin'," he grinned.

"My parents don't believe girls should marry too young," she offered. "They're very close and so right for each other, so I'm sure it's true. I think Mama was about Sarah's age and Daddy a couple of years older

61

when they married."

"Good officer, Major Landis," Jeb informed the trouble-shooters. "Got promoted a couple years back, and he sure earned it."

"Daddy says every officer of the Eighth could learn a lot from you when it comes to tracking," she said.

"Your daddy's no liar," said Jeb. "I dunno how old I am, but I figure I'm too old to be modest."

"And I think . . . " She eyed Larry and Stretch very seriously, "every officer, NCO and trooper of the Eighth could learn a lot from you — when it comes to fighting."

"C'mon now, Miss Naomi," frowned Stretch. "Big cavalry outfit don't need no lessons from the likes of us."

"You were very young, weren't you?" she said. "Younger than I am, just boys, when you fought in the war?"

"Didn't have our full growth, but we were tall already." Larry grinned reminiscently and sipped coffee. "Maybe the recruitin' sergeant was thinkin' of sendin' us back to school, but he didn't."

"I guess we were old enough to fight," mused Stretch.

"Must've been," said Larry.

"Sure," said Stretch. "Wasn't but a few weeks later we got into the action. Didn't feel good at first, Union artillery blastin' all around our outfit, musket balls whinin' past our heads. But we got the hang of it, huh runt?"

"Just had to learn," shrugged Larry.

"The hard way," suggested Jeb.

"Sure enough," agreed Larry. "The hard way."

Sensing Naomi was becoming a touch maudlin on their account, he and Stretch cleaned their plates, drained their cups and set them on the tray; the sympathy of well-meaning women, especially the younger ones, tended to unsettle them. Jeb had finished his supper. The girl rose, balancing the tray, and asked, "Could something happen tonight?"

"Too early I reckon," said Jeb.

"Sometime tomorrow's my guess. Meantime, everybody oughta get plenty sleep. When the time comes, we all gotta be sharp."

"It was nice talking to you," she murmured.

"Likewise," said Larry.

After she left them, Jeb commented, "Strangest durn thing, the way a man can ruffle a female's feathers. You boys hit it off good with the Landis kid, but it ain't like that with Miss Sarah, huh? Always was high-falutin' that'un, but why d'you suppose she acts so vinegary around you?"

"Damned if I know, Jeb," said Larry, getting to his feet. "But I ain't frettin' about it. Got more important stuff on my mind than the colonel's daughter." He moved to the pointed tops of the stockade and stared into the distance. "Flat out there, and we can see a long ways. Moonlight's real bright."

Planting himself beside his partner, Stretch observed, "No cover for miles. If they rush us for starters, it'll be a turkey-shoot." He glanced at Jeb. "He's that crazy, this Corsario?"

"He's a wild'un," growled Jeb. "Don't care how many men he loses. Life's cheap to him. It'll pleasure him to kill as many of us as he can, then grab some women and kids and leave some kinda message for the colonel — the women and kids for as many horses and guns, as much ammunition as he demands."

"If it all went his way, how would the colonel act?" asked Stretch.

"Tall boy," said Jeb, "I just dunno — wouldn't even try to guess."

Far to the north, the 8th Cavalry was on the move, their commanding officer and his aides reasoning they could travel faster in the lower temperatures of the night; easier on the horses. In the lead, the two majors, Richards and Landis, were flanking Colonel Delmer and trading hunches with him.

3

The Subject is Courage

JOHN DELMER was tall, spare of build, but blunt-featured, his mustache and short beard neatly tended. A veteran soldier dedicated to the cause now adhered to by all army units of the frontier, the protection of civilians, he believed he was headed into battle with the Comancheros. At Rowansburg, his regiment would bring relief to townfolk valiantly holding out against Corsario's superior force; he would mount an attack on the raiders and the Southwest would be rid of its greatest scourge once and for all.

"Once and for all," he said emphatically. "That damn butcher has run roughshod for far too long. He has to be stopped and, as I've always insisted, the Eighth is committed to that task."

"I wonder if Rowansburg's doctors are surviving," reflected Richards, the heavyset surgeon of the regiment. "It's possible, John, you'll see little of me after the battle is won. I anticipate I'll be attending a great many civilians as well as our own casualties."

"Too bad tradition has to be observed," the blondly-handsome Major Ira Landis remarked with a genial grin. "Your Beth is a mighty competent nurse, George. Well, it's a tradition and a logical one, no women accompanying the regiment into combat. I certainly wouldn't appreciate having Ellie along."

"Beth has learned a lot," agreed Richards. "Well, typical army surgeon's wife after all. But the really fast learner is young Ainsworth. That boy continues to impress me with his aptitude. What could've possessed him to enlist in the US Cavalry, when it's patently obvious he should be in medical school?"

"He should be in the guardhouse with those six insubordinate trouble-makers, Yarrow, Gleddon and their cronies," scowled Delmer. "Thunderation! Any soldier found sleeping on guard duty is not worth his salt. If it hadn't been for your interceding on his behalf, George . . . "

"I should shoulder some of the blame," said Richards. "My mistake was lending him Coburg's essays on surgical procedure. That work is three inches thick. He was absorbed in it — I guess it fascinated him — for five hours before he went to his guard post. Mental exhaustion, John. Small wonder he flopped."

"Otherwise, his record is clean I believe," said Landis. "That was his first offence?"

"It had better be his last," declared the colonel, staring ahead. "Damn! This is as fast as we can move, and who knows what's happening at Rowansburg at this moment? The deputy said Corsario's men were closing in on the basin when he started for the fort."

"Civilians can be resourceful in

time of crisis," soothed Landis. "I'm sure Sheriff Kingsmill has organized barricades, placement of provisions and ammunition . . . "

"Probably confined the women and children to cellars," opined Richards. "Take heart, John. The Comancheros won't have it all their own way. Rowansburg folk will put up stiff resistance."

"Overthrowing Corsario's band is a job for the cavalry," insisted Delmer. "Lord, how I wish he'd struck closer to headquarters."

"Will he and his kind never learn?" frowned Landis. "This was their country but, with white settlement on the increase for better than twenty-five years, they must realize we're here to stay."

"No matter how many Comanches follow him, no matter how many murderous Mexicans and renegade whites, he can't maraud and pillage much longer," said Richards. "There'll be a day of reckoning. If this hasn't occurred to him, maybe he's as demented as border folk believe him to be."

"Scum of his calibre always meet a violent end," muttered Delmer.

"I suppose that's the way they want to go," shrugged Landis.

"A blaze of glory — from his point of view," Delmer said bitterly. "Hoping to take a lot of white men with him when his time comes." He glanced over his shoulder. "Is that supply wagon keeping up, or falling back?"

"Don't worry, John," said Landis. "If Sergeant Breen's team were lagging, we'd know by now."

The column pushed on northward while, at Fort Mitchum, women of the regiment and the men on guard on the parapets continued to wait it out — waiting for the inevitable.

Trooper Ainsworth had finished the duty given him by Sergeant Mulligan and was back in the infirmary. Also present, storing improvised bandaging, were Beth Richards, Chloe Toone and the colonel's daughter. Ainsworth was keeping to himself, swabbing the operating table. He had already swept and mopped the floor; the infirmary was spotless. Doggedly, he avoided Sarah's probing gaze. His sixth sense warned him she would at any moment utter a cutting remark. When it came, he resisted the impulse to flinch.

"*Some* good may come of the impending crisis," she remarked to the other women. "It should cure Trooper Ainsworth of his tendency to sleep on guard duty."

"Now, Sarah dear . . . " began Chloe Toone.

"He'll no doubt feel safer here — away from the fighting," Sarah coldly continued. "His excuse for being in charge of the infirmary is thin, to say the least. You, Mrs Richards, are probably more efficient at treating wounds than he could ever be."

"It's hardly likely I could have done more for Captain Blore than this young man," argued the surgeon's wife.

"Thank you, Mrs Richards," Ainsworth acknowledged.

"True anyway," she assured him. "I'm not patronizing you. I was on hand, as you'll recall. Excellent work, Trooper, the setting of the captain's leg, the binding of his ribs."

"And requiring little courage," jibed Sarah.

Ainsworth turned from the operating table to face the women.

"Permission to speak in my defence?" he politely requested.

"How formal," smiled Sarah.

"I'm in the company of my commanding officer's daughter and the wives of two officers," he pointed out.

"Speak freely," invited Beth Richards.

"By all means," urged Chloe Toone.

"I'm not a coward — at least I don't think I am," he said quietly. "It's just that I have to agree with the opinions of Sergeant Mulligan and those cowhands who arrived with Mister Penn. I'll be of greater use treating our wounded than on the parapet."

"That remains to be seen," Sarah retorted.

"Well . . . " He shrugged and turned away, "that's all I wanted to say."

Secretly, he chided himself. His emotions should be under tighter control. What use to yearn for this fair-haired, so imperious beauty? How could he compete with the dashing and handsome Lieutenant Grescoe for her affections when he could not even earn her respect?

"He outranks you in every way," he reflected. "You're a fool to have fallen in love with her. There's just *no* chance for you."

He could only give himself credit for realistic resignation. He did realize it was hopeless, and wasn't this better than deluding himself, daydreaming about her?

Polly Glynn, Elmira Landis and Leona Harrington were congratulating themselves on an efficient job of converting a barracks to a dormitory for the children. The makeshift partition would hold and now the small fry were bedded down, boys to the right, girls to the left. Before extinguishing lamps, the women did some tucking in, murmuring words of comfort.

Were the children aware of the prevailing situation? How could it be otherwise at Fort Mitchum, where kids overheard the conversation of their elders, where news of any kind travelled fast?

Polly Glynn doubted George Richards Junior would appreciate being tucked in, but paused by his bunk for a few words. He was the eldest boy of this military community, twelve and a half years old. The surgeon major and his spouse were more amused than dismayed that their first-born had inherited neither their looks nor their temperament. He was homely, tousle-haired and gruff-voiced. His eight-year-old sister had her mother's coloring and her father's nose and promised to be as practical and as strong-nerved as the hard-to-faze Beth.

Junior tended to be short on patience, and proved it when Lieutenant Glynn's wife adjusted his pillow.

"I oughtn't be here," he growled.

"Bedtime, George," she smiled. "Now where on earth else should you be at this time of night?"

"Up there on a catwalk, gettin' ready to fight Comancheros," he complained. "Think I can't do my share, Mrs Glynn ma'am?"

"You're too young," she said.

"Pa taught me pistol shootin'," he argued.

"That was just target shooting with your daddy cocking his revolver for you," she reminded him. "It's not as easy, George dear, to hit moving targets — human targets. That's work for grown men."

"I'm sick of bein' too young," he grouched. "Movin' targets? Think I don't know what you mean? Raiders on horses. I bet I could hit one of 'em, maybe more'n one."

"Your dear parents would be terribly

upset if they knew you had such notions," she chided. "Now you be obedient like the other children, be an example to them. That's the best way you young ones can help. And we're all counting on you. Remember that, George."

"Aw, shoot," he grunted.

She smiled and withdrew with the other women.

Toward midnight, heavy footsteps were heard on steps leading up to parapets. Troopers Yarrow, Sykes and Frost came trudging to the south wall to relieve Jeb, the trouble-shooters and Sergeants Elvy and Ulric. They hefted three rifles apiece to add to the armory already stacked on the catwalk; bringing up the rear, Frost also toted a box of ammunition on his shoulder.

Loudly, Yarrow announced, "Mulligan says for you jaspers to catch some sleep."

"Make that *Sergeant* Mulligan," Elvy reprimanded. "And you don't have to holler, Trooper."

"How long'll you boys be standin' guard?" asked Stretch.

"Till sun-up," said Frost. "Red and Biff and Dan'll take over from us."

"Every son's gotta get as much shut-eye as he can *while* he can, Mulligan says," growled Sykes. "Party'll start some time after sun-up, right ol' Jeb?"

"Right," said Jeb, yawning. "And don't call me old, Trooper, 'less you crave for me to kick your ass off of this catwalk."

"You always was a salty ol' cuss, Jeb," grinned Yarrow. "Hey, it's good you're with us. Like ol' times, huh?"

"Well," said Jeb. "Gimme a choice, I'd as soon take my chances here than way southeast where I could get run down by Comancheros and lose my hair and what it's growin' out of."

"When it's all over, I'll make you a present of Corsario's scalp," offered Yarrow.

"Fight as brave as you talk and you'll do fine," said Jeb. He looked at the drifters. "You bucks ain't been off your feet since we rid in here. Bone-weary men don't fight as good as when they're rested."

"We know that, Jeb," Larry assured him.

"Sure," nodded Jeb. "Who'd know better'n you fiddlefoots? So lets find us some bunks and call it a day."

The veteran warriors didn't even bother to light a lamp. Entering a barracks-room, they found their way to empty bunks by feel, squatted to remove hats and sidearms and spurs, but not boots, then flopped and sank into slumber.

★ ★ ★

In dawn's early light they advanced from the southeast, a large force of Comancheros, a cross-section of full-bloods, half-breeds, Mexican bandits and renegade whites.

To the fore, the infamous Corsario was flanked by the leering Sam Gillis, the border desperado who had thrown in with the leader of the Comancheros, the cunning rogue whose shrewd ruse had emptied Fort Mitchum of all but one of its officers, all but three NCOs and all but seven troopers.

"They fell for it," he gleefully assured Corsario. "After I quit the fort, I took cover and watched the whole outfit, all them Long Knives, ride out and head north in one helluva hurry. Couldn't be enough guns left at Mitchum to put up any kinda fight."

Flanking Corsario on his right side was the pudgy Luis Henriquez, whose band of bandidos had boosted the raiding party by one third. Henriquez had plenty to show for his gluttony, a double chin, a round belly emphasized by a scarlet sash and a shellbelt double-holstered. Aiming a yellow-toothed leer at his new leader, he predicted, "It will be as you wish, compadre. Today we will take many women, the wives of the soldados, many ninos too, si? For them, the Long Knives will give mucho caballos and weapons."

"They will give what I demand, the soldados," muttered Corsario. He was taller than his henchmen and his was the face of evil, swarthy, hawk-like, a scar extending from left cheek-bone to jowl. He was stripped to the waist and his chest war-painted. His headgear was a sombrero, seven feathers fixed to its band. "Their commandante, the one called Delmer, will mourn the loss of the women — and he will obey."

"You're headin' up a big outfit now," said Gillis. "But with all them cavalry horses and hardware, it's gonna be bigger. By damn, we're gonna control the whole southwest!"

And so, confident of any easy victory, the raiders moved northwest toward Fort Mitchum, which was now astir.

Well rested, full of breakfast, Larry and Stretch inspected preparations around the fort's buildings before making for the south parapet. They hefted their own Winchesters, remembering many more loaded weapons and an ample supply of ammunition were positioned at strategic points along every catwalk. Pails of water were very much in evidence. The children had been fed and were restricted to Barracks Number 4, two women with them, the other women behind the locked door of the administration building. Stretch glimpsed some of them watching from windows.

"Everybody's got the feelin' all hell's gonna bust loose purty soon," he remarked to his partner as they crossed the parade ground. "And I got it too."

"And me," nodded Larry.

"We'll sight 'em today, huh?" prodded Stretch.

"That's Jeb's figurin', and I go along with him," said Larry.

The taller drifter remarked, when they were nearing a flight of steps, "Big'un this time, runt. Won't be no straggle of Injuns headed our way. Big raidin' party, likely hundreds of 'em."

"That's how it'll be," agreed Larry.

"We got somethin' to be thankful for, amigo."

"Meanin'?" asked Stretch.

"The Eighth Cavalry took plenty ammunition to Rowansburg," said Larry. "But they left plenty behind, didn't empty the armory. Ain't near as many of us as'll come a'raidin', but we got firepower aplenty."

Martin Ainsworth positioned himself in the open entrance to the infirmary and stared across the compound. Watching the tall men climb to the catwalk, he felt a stirring of excitement. Fear? No, he assured himself. His nerves were steadier than the woman he loved could imagine. Anticipation? Yes, that was it. Anticipation, resignation and willingness. Soon enough, the Comancheros would appear. From the south, he assumed, because the defenders were manning that side of the stockade. Soon enough, he would be tending casualties. So be it. He was ready, dressings, bandages, antiseptic, water to be brought to the

82

boil for sterilizing surgical instruments. If he had to work fast, he would remember one of Major Richard's remarks; whiskey, any alcohol, was almost as reliable as sterilizer.

"God, guide my hands," he whispered. "Don't let me fail any of them."

Finishing their ascent, the drifters traded nods with Jeb and Mulligan. They were all here, all the able-bodied, heavily armed and ready for anything, Sergeants Elvey and Ulric with them this side of the gate, Troopers Yarrow, Sykes, O'Curran, Janney, Frost and Gleddon lined right of it, all staring south with rifles at the ready.

"You'd best hear my plan," Mulligan told the trouble-shooters. "Ain't complicated. If they start a charge across the flats, we open up soon as they're in range, down as many as we can . . . "

"*That* sure ain't complicated," grinned Stretch.

"If they spread 'emselves and try surroundin' the fort, we'll have to

83

split up," continued Mulligan. "So there'll be riflemen on the east, west and rear parapets. We keep scorin' on the bastards, they'll think twice about tryin' to close in on us. Sound good to you, Valentine?"

"Best we can do for starters," shrugged Larry. "I guess all you soldier-boys'll remember to raise sights. A rifle slug travels a long ways. The more of 'em we can stop at long range, the less of 'em'll get close enough to be a blame nuisance." He glanced to the weapons stacked close to the other sergeants. "How many shotguns you got there?"

"Half-dozen," replied Elvey.

"And plenty spare shells," growled Ulric. "Don't fret yourself, cowboy. We're savin' the scatterguns for them that get close enough to be fazed by buckshot."

"Ain't frettin' one little bit, Sarge," Larry assured him. "Plain enough my partner and me're in good company."

"We're kinda glad Jeb and you boys're with us," Elvey said amiably.

From the catwalk beyond the gates, Red Gleddon called a taunt.

"Sorry you hung around, Trouble–Shooter?"

"Damn right, Red," answered Larry. "Scared clear down to my boots."

"Me too," announced Stretch. "Look how I'm shakin'."

Yarrow and the others chuckled. Gleddon glowered across at Larry and growled a threatening reminder.

"When it's all over, me and you got unfinished business, hot shot."

"When it's all over," nodded Larry.

The wind was blowing from the south. Jeb was squinting through his spyglass and Pike Yarrow sniffing.

"Sonofabitch," he said, nudging Biff Janney. "I can smell Comancheros."

Jeb was making the same claim to Mulligan and the drifters, still peering through his telescope.

"They got a special stink."

"See anything?" demanded Mulligan.

"Not even their dust," mumbled Jeb. "But they're comin', betcha lives."

"Soon!" Mulligan called to the other defenders. "Stand fast — but don't get fired up! No shootin' till I give the word! Adjust sights for maximum range! Maybe I'll wait for their first warlike move — and maybe I won't!"

Eyes fixed southward, they waited. Fifteen minutes passed before the dust, a long line of it, was visible. Ten more minutes and, out of the dust and the shimmering heat waves, the great force appeared.

The raiders were a long way off, but the old scout wasn't about to mistake them for non-hostiles. He set his spyglass aside, readied a rifle and told Mulligan, "It's them, comin' on slow. I spotted Corsario."

"He's the one I'd make my first target," Mulligan said wistfully. "But . . . "

"Uh huh," grunted Jeb. "You couldn't be so lucky. When they come a chargin', him and his under-chiefs — like that bandido Henriquez — gonna fall back and let their first wave do all the fightin'."

The trouble-shooters took up positions and readied their Winchesters, adjusting their sights. Still a lot of ground between the fort and the attack force, so they didn't hesitate to build and light cigarettes.

"One damn ruckus after another," drawled Stretch. "That's all we get."

"Beats raisin' chickens, growin' fat and lazy," Larry philosophized.

"I guess," shrugged Stretch.

Mulligan's command had been audible to some. Ainsworth again appeared in the infirmary doorway as Captain Blore emerged from his quarters with his wife trying to restrain him. He was in uniform, sidearms strapped on, using his crutch and cursing.

"Tom — you can't . . . !" cried Marj.

"Mrs Blore's right, sir," Ainsworth called to him.

"Confound it, they're about to attack!" protested Blore.

"Soon, I'm sure," nodded Ainsworth. "I heard Sergeant Mulligan's alert. But you can't climb to the parapet, not in your condition. Direct our defence from where you are, sir. The sergeant will hear you."

"You know he won't," retorted Blore. "It's only a matter of time before all any of us will hear is gunfire."

"Sergeant Mulligan's a combat veteran," Marj urgently reminded him. "Even if you could reach the parapets — and you couldn't — you could do no more than the sergeant. He'll remember all your orders, and follow them."

"I resent feeling so damn *useless*," complained Blore.

"Sir, if you tried to cross the compound, I'd be forced to restrain you," warned Ainsworth. "Please don't do that to me."

"Damn the luck," scowled Blore. "*Damn* the luck!"

Fifteen more minutes and the Comancheros were clearly visible. Horses were milling now and war whoops rising on the morning air.

"Well now, Sarge," Larry drawled. "I

reckon you know what that caterwaulin' means."

"Their way of announcin' 'emselves, Mulligan," declared Elvey.

"Hollerin' of how they're gonna take scalps," growled Jeb.

"Sounds plumb unfriendly," remarked Stretch.

"Insultin'," scowled Ulric. "Hey, Irish, I call that provocation."

"Indeed it is," decided Mulligan. "A declaration of war, bedad, so I'll not wait for 'em to fire the first shot." He raised his voice again. "We ain't waitin' for 'em to start for us! Choose targets . . . !"

"And don't all choose the same damn target for hell's sakes!" bellowed Larry.

"Sights adjusted?" demanded Mulligan.

"All set!" called Janney. "I'm all lined up on a whoopin' buck!"

"At long range . . . !" yelled Mulligan. "Open fire!"

No defender triggered impulsively. Every man on the south parapet took accurate aim before firing. A dozen rifles barked and, as the shots echoed across the flats, exactly that number of whooping braves parted company with their horses the hard way.

"Keep it up!" urged Larry, as the charge began.

The first wave advanced at a headlong rush, Comanches loosing arrows that would fall short, others discharging muskets. In a matter of moments, bullets were raining about the stockade, but the defenders held their positions, aiming with care, triggering and scoring. The clamor of gunfire, the screams of Comancheros mortally wounded, caused the younger of the children in Barracks 4 to wince and press hands to ears. Chloe Toone and Naomi Landis moved among them, murmuring comfortingly, forcing smiles of reassurance. George Richards Junior was peering out a window.

In the administration building, the other women were assembled in the parlor of the commanding officer's quarters. They looked at Mattie Delmer for encouragement. She nodded calmly.

"Patience, my dears," she said. "We may be sure every man on the south parapet is doing his duty — and giving our uninvited visitors a hot reception."

Matching the older woman's calm, Leona Harrington reminded her friends, "Not their first taste of battle. They're veterans, all of them."

Predictably, the tallest of the defenders were wreaking havoc on fast-advancing horsemen, their Winchesters barking relentlessly, their eyes, trigger-fingers and nerves rock-steady. Beside the trouble-shooters, Jeb was doing his share and then some.

Scoring on a Mexican, Larry saw him pitch from his mount and fall before the forehooves of an animal straddled by a Comanche bowman. The horse, carried on by its impetus, tripped over the Mexican's body and fell and rolled, crushing its screaming rider.

Stretch set his empty rifle aside,

took up another and resumed shooting, toppling three riders in rapid succession. Sights were being readjusted; the attackers were coming in close. Then, abruptly, three other groups appeared, making for the east and west flats. Mulligan didn't need to give the command. Larry and Stretch ran for the east catwalk, Gleddon and Janney for the west side and Frost following, his destination the rear wall, in case the attackers reached the area north.

With so many loaded weapons close at hand, the defenders of the east and west walls had an edge on horsemen attempting to circle the fort. The trouble-shooters again wreaked havoc; Gleddon and Janney rendered horse after horse riderless, rarely missing their targets.

They were drawing fire, but the shooting of the Mexicans and Comanches was ragged. On the north catwalk, Frost waited for others to appear, but sighted only two, both of whom he slew; he only fired twice.

Then Gleddon's luck ran out. A musket ball creased his right side and spun him off-balance. Had he plunged from the catwalk, he might have broken his neck. But, when he fell, he crashed onto steps. Swearing luridly, he tumbled down, back-somersaulting before hitting the dust.

At once, Ainsworth began a dash to where the big redhead had fallen. Arrows rained into the compound, several embedding right and left of him as, bent double, he hurried on. Reaching the still swearing trooper, he began lifting him.

"You ain't got muscle enough to tote me!" Gleddon snarled at him.

"Don't take any bets," muttered Ainsworth.

Gleddon loosed a howl of pain as the younger trooper raised him and draped him across his shoulders. Then he was stumbling for the infirmary entrance zig-zag fashion, hoping against hope neither he nor his hefty burden would be struck by arrows. One embedded in the wall left of the doorway, quivering, just as Ainsworth toted Gleddon across the threshold. The Indian who had loosed that one was now dying, hurtling over his pony's rump with a bullet triggered by Mulligan in his heart.

"Patch me fast — I gotta get back up there!" Gleddon gasped as Ainsworth deposited him on the operating table.

"Hold still while I examine you," ordered Ainsworth.

"You ain't a real doc," scowled Gleddon.

"I'm all you've got, so do yourself a favor," retorted Ainsworth. "Don't make this any rougher on either of us." He rolled Gleddon's blouse and undershirt up to his armpits to examine the bullet gash, then hastily checked his limbs. "Left forearm broken. All right, first I douse the creased ribs to stop the bleeding. This'll hurt." He held a bottle to Gleddon's mouth. "Three good gulps. It's the good stuff, Gleddon, Major Richard's own bourbon."

He worked swiftly. His patient lost blood before he was able to stem the flow and get to work on the broken arm. It didn't surprise him that Gleddon stayed conscious while he set and splinted the broken arm; the big redhead was so stubborn.

"I'm righthanded," he mumbled. "Can't fire a rifle, but I can get a six-shooter and . . . "

"Later maybe, not rightaway, not till I say so," frowned Ainsworth. "Next I have to dress the gunshot wound and fix a sling for the arm, then I'm putting you on a cot."

"The hell you are!" protested Gleddon.

"You've lost blood, so you have to rest and take nourishment to regain your strength," declared Ainsworth. "Damn it, Gleddon, don't you realize bleeding weakens a man?"

"I ain't weak — who're you callin' weak?" blustered Gleddon. "You're the only chicken-livered jasper in this man's out-fit!"

"I won't argue with you," said Ainsworth. "I'll just let you prove it — to yourself. Then maybe you'll take my word for it." He made short work of plastering a dressing to the side wound, fixed a sling to support the broken arm, then growled an invitation. "You can get up now. Come on, Gleddon. Off the table."

The big redhead swung his legs to the floor, lowered himself to his feet and, wearing a puzzled expression, practically collapsed against Ainsworth.

"Damn and blast . . . !"

"Right arm over my shoulder — and hang on," instructed Ainsworth. "There's a cot just over here. Any more arguments?"

"Head's all — fuzzy . . . "

"All you need is time and rest. Come on now, easy does it."

From the parapets, the defenders kept up a steady burst of accurate fire at riders circling the stockade. Those who tried to move in close got the worst of it. Horse after horse lost its rider during this first assault and more than one of the hold-outs almost lost their lives.

Larry heard his partner's yell and darted a glance his way. To his relief, Stretch hadn't stopped a bullet, but he was wild-eyed and cussing lustily and hatless, his holed Stetson sailing above the compound, dropping.

"Sonofabitch!" he raged.

"Close, but not close enough," Larry called to him encouragingly. "Your head ain't bloody, amigo, so you're still with me. And we still got a lot of shootin' to do."

Fury didn't affect the taller drifter's aim. He lined on another rider, a Comanche drawing back his bowstring to loose an arrow. With the bark of his rifle, the redman plunged from his mount; the arrow roared to the sky. Simultaneously, Larry drilled a rifle-brandishing Mexican.

The next defender to suffer pain was Trooper O'Curran, who dropped his rifle and roared and reeled. Sykes made a grab for him, caught him by an arm and prevented his toppling from the catwalk. He could see blood staining the whole right side of O'Curran's face, his contorted face; the tough Irishman was in agony.

"Slug nicked your ear, Dan," he said. "Press your kerchief to it and make for the steps. You gotta get to the infirmary fast!"

When O'Curran finished his descent and bee-lined for the infirmary entrance, Beth Richards was approaching from the opposite direction. By now, she was thinking, Martin Ainsworth probably needed help. Or moral support.

4

'They'll Be Back'

SEEING O'Curran arrive on his own two feet, half his face and the whole right side of his tunic blood-soaked, Ainsworth reached for a cloth and a bowl of water and gestured to a chair.

"Sit. What is it? Two wounds? You couldn't be carrying a bullet."

"Hurts like hell!" wailed O'Curran, as the surgeon major's wife bustled in. "Slug only nicked my ear — but it feels like its afire!"

"A lady present," Ainsworth cautioned, and began swabbing blood away.

"Beggin' your pardon, ma'am," groaned O'Curran

"As the major would say, cuss all you want," invited Beth, moving closer.

"We oughtn't be floppin' here,

99

O'Curran," Gleddon complained from his cot.

"Speak for your consarn self!" retorted O'Curran.

Ainsworth cleared the area about the damaged ear. He and Beth traded grim stares.

"Most of the lobe," he muttered, as if she hadn't noticed. "Gone. Just shot away."

"If you cauterize . . . " she began.

"Yes," he nodded. "The pain would be intense. I'd have to administer ether first."

"You have an alternative," she reminded him. "A generous application will stem the bleeding. Your decision, Trooper Ainsworth."

"The jar numbered . . . " he frowned.

"Three . . . " she said.

"Three, three, seven," he nodded. "Just as effective, and easier on the patient. O'Curran, hold this cloth to your ear."

Beth Richards offered no further advice. She stood by and observed and this didn't seem to bother Ainsworth, absorbed in his work. He dashed to a cabinet, returned with the jar and dabbed a generous portion of the substance to the damaged ear, muttering reassuringly to O'Curran, promising his pain would soon ease. He then prepared a dressing, smeared it with balm and secured it with plaster.

"That'll do it," the patient said impatiently.

"I have to tell you what I told Gleddon," said Ainsworth. "You bled profusely and blood loss causes inertia."

"If that's catchin', keep him away from me," growled Gleddon.

Beth approved Ainsworth's involuntary grin.

"No, it's not contagious, but you're fellow-sufferers for the time being," he said. "I can't discharge either of you till you've rested and taken nourishment. Take my word, you'd be useless out there."

"The other one?" asked Beth.

"Left arm broken, ma'am, two

dented ribs," reported Ainsworth. "I'll help you up now, O'Curran. Move slowly. You're a cot case till I say otherwise."

"If neither of them has thrown up . . . " said Beth.

"No indications of nausea," Ainsworth assured her.

"They should have something as quickly as possible," she decided. "Mrs Landis has beefbroth heating. I'll fetch it at once, also a platter of bread and a pot of coffee. I believe the major would recommend you spike their coffee with whiskey. For medicinal purposes, Trooper Ainsworth."

"Ma'am . . . " he began as she made for the door.

"I'll be careful," she said over her shoulder. "Your patients need feeding."

While reaching for another rifle, Larry glimpsed Sarah Delmer and two other women. They were on the catwalks, moving on all fours, hastily but efficiently reloading discarded weapons. He cursed bitterly and ordered them to get below. They ignored him, so he grimaced, raised himself again, felt the wind of the arrow that sped past his face and downed the Comanche who had fired it.

Sergeant Elvey had bounded to the west catwalk to replace Gleddon. Sykes was now with Frost on the north side, both of them directing rapid fire at still circling riders.

Ten minutes later, Mulligan bellowed a command.

"Hold your fire! They're pullin' back."

"It's a retreat," Elvey muttered to Jeb.

Larry and Stretch weren't about to relax their vigilance. With Mulligan's approval, they urged their companions to keep their weapons cocked and at the ready.

"Never trust a Comanchero!" warned Larry. "Even when he's retreatin'!"

The fort was no longer encircled. The raiders were retreating to the south, some pausing to aid wounded companeros, but leaving the dead where they had fallen, others concentrated on herding riderless horses away. Riding drag of the herders was a Mexican straddling a roan and holding aloft a lance to which he had fixed a white cloth. The men of Fort Mitchum respected this improvised flag of truce until they were treated to proof of the fanaticism of south of the border bandidos who had allied themselves to Corsario.

Still holding the truce flag high, the Mexican waited till the horses had been mustered and were being driven south, then quickly turned in his saddle with his free hand full of six-gun and a leer creasing his swarthy visage. Maybe he had cocked the pistol, but he wasn't given time to pull trigger. Three rifles barked from the south parapet, three bullets struck the leering target; a fourth severed the lance. The body went to ground in a bloody, lifeless heap.

Larry and Stretch set their rifles aside

and made their way along the catwalk to the group bunched left of the gates.

"Sure, they're retreatin' now," scowled Mulligan. "But they'll be back."

"Bet your stripes on it, Emmett," growled Jeb.

Mulligan drew his gaze from the southbound Comancheros and scanned the catwalks.

"Ain't worth a roll call, but it's regulation," he told the drifters. "All right, we got three civilians and three sergeants as healthy as when the attack started — don't nobody ask me why." He raised his voice. "Janney! I don't see Gleddon nor O'Curran!"

"In the infirmary!" Janney reported. "Red got creased, might have some other hurts too!"

"Slug took off some of O'Curran's ear!" announced Sykes. "They ain't dead, but they're sure hurtin'!"

"Call it a miracle we only got two wounded, Emmett," said Ulric. "Must've been Corsario's whole swarm hit us."

"Includin' the reinforcements he was waitin' for," opined Jeb.

"Looks like we whittled 'em down some," drawled Stretch, scanning the fort's surroundings, the strewn dead.

"I'll not call it a miracle," said Mulligan. "They attacked from open ground. We had cover, they had none. Sure there's a lotta stiffs out there, but Corsario don't count his losses, not with as many more backin' him."

When only dust was visible south of the fort, Larry nudged Stretch and urged Mulligan, "Have a couple troopers open the gates for us."

"What . . . ?" blinked Mulligan.

"They don't have to open 'em wide," said Stretch. "Just a couple feet, we so can slip through."

"We're goin' out there," explained Larry.

"What in blazes for?" gasped Elvey.

"Whatever hardware we can find — as much as we can tote," Larry said calmly. "No muskets, but repeaters, sure, and bandoleers, pistols . . . "

"We're fixed pretty good for arms and ammo," protested Elvey.

"But we can't even guess how soon the regiment'll come home," countered Larry. "Nor how many more attacks we'll have to fight off meantime. Any hombre don't believe we need every weapon we can find, he ain't thinkin' straight. Go on, Sarge. Give the order."

Mulligan gave the order. The trouble-shooters made for the nearest steps while Sykes and Janney vacated a catwalk.

"Best we get ready to cover them rover boys," advised Jeb.

"Nothin's movin' out there," argued Elvey.

"We're up against Comancheros, not gentleman-soldiers," retorted Jeb.

After slipping out of the fort, the drifters separated, Larry making for the west side, Stretch for the east. The taller trouble-shooter worked quickly. Soon, he was hurling rifles up and over the stockade, and every weapon clattering to the catwalk or pitching into the compound was of the type on issue to the 8th Cavalry, a Winchester. He gathered bandoleers and several pistols, while his partner imitated his actions west of the stockade. They joined up on the north side to add another half-dozen rifles and as many pistols to their haul. They also kept a sharp lookout for potentially dangerous wounded, but none of the sprawled figures stirred.

Rounding the south corner, they began selecting and gathering weapons dropped during the first charge, guns and bandoleers. Larry uncocked the Colt tugged from the dead hand of the treacherous Mexican and rammed it into his waistband, while Sykes and Janney watched from the partly open gates.

The troopers took delivery of arms fetched to them by the tall men, who then moved away to resume their search. Stretch was hefting four rifles, Larry draping a couple of bandoleers over his shoulder; their backs were turned to the huddled figures of three redmen when Janney yelled, "Behind you!"

The men up top couldn't fire at the rising figure for fear of hitting their intended victims. The braves showed body and leg wounds, but each aimed a lance. So swift was the reaction of the trouble-shooters, the watchers couldn't catch every detail. Stretch dropped his load as his partner filled his hand. With the boom of Larry's Colt, a Comanche died with a .45 slug in his head. Stretch's lightning double-draw, the roaring of his matched six-guns, ensured neither of the other redmen would ever again hurl a lance. They shuddered and sprawled on their backs, blood welling from the centre of their chests.

"Hell's bells!" breathed Ulric. "Did you see . . . ?"

"We all saw them drifters gun down three that were playin' possum," muttered Mulligan.

"What we *didn't* see was how fast

109

they got their hoglegs outa leather," Jeb said soberly.

The tall men made two more deliveries to the troopers at the gate. Larry then glanced southward. Still gripping his Colt, he called to Mulligan.

"We're gonna be out here a mite longer."

"Might be some more of 'em still live enough to throw a knife or a tomahawk," said Stretch. "We just learned us a hard lesson."

"Better lock them gates just in case," advised Larry.

The tall men spent another hour out there; it took them that long to ensure no other redmen were lying doggo. They were let in by Sykes and Janney, who resecured the gates. Elvey and Ulric undertook the necessary chore of checking all weapons once used by Comancheros to ensure they were in good working condition.

Slowly, the as-yet unscathed trouble-shooters made for a well. En route, Stretch retrieved his Stetson and, before redonning it, scowled at the two holes, points of entry and exit, in the crown. They worked the windlass, drew up the filled pail. Larry half-emptied it over his head; Stretch upended it over his own. Dripping, they surveyed each other.

"Well," said Larry. "Not this time, huh?"

"Maybe next time they hit us," shrugged Stretch. "Our luck's got to run out sooner or later."

"I'd settle for later," Larry confided. "They're friends of ours now, the folks here. Be kind of fittin' if they come through this ruckus alive and no woman stolen by Corsario. I guess what I crave most is to be alive enough to see the regiment come hightailin' it back and send them Comancheros runnin'."

"That's gonna be somethin' to see," agreed Stretch. "Worth stayin' alive for?"

"Anything is," said Larry.

They returned to the south catwalk to rejoin Jeb and Mulligan. A short time later, Polly Glynn and Naomi

Landis appeared, each toting trays bearing steaming coffeepots and tin cups. They climbed to the catwalks to move among the men, who gratefully accepted coffee as they liked it, hot, strong and black.

"The ladies okay, ma'am?" Mulligan politely enquired of Polly.

"In good spirits, the children too," she said. "I declare, Sergeant Mulligan, our brave protectors will be the heroes of the regiment. Can you imagine how the colonel will feel when he returns, when we tell him how just thirteen of you held so many Comancheros at bay?"

"I guess you and the other ladies don't need to be told it ain't over," frowned Mulligan.

"We realize they'll attack again," she said. "But we're in no doubt you'll hold them back." She nodded emphatically. "Our faith in you and these other brave men never wavers."

When every man had accounted for his fill of coffee and the women had left them, Mulligan traded stares with Jeb and wondered, "How're we gonna live up to what them women think of us?"

"We keep on doin' the same damn thing," shrugged the old scout.

"They keep comin', we keep fightin' 'em off," drawled Stretch. "It could get monotonous."

Mulligan lit a cigar, his moody gaze on the area south.

"Best go talk to the captain presently," he muttered. "Jeb, if you had to make a guess . . . ?"

"Mightn't rush us again today," opined Jeb. "But tonight could be good for 'em and bad for us. If it's dark, they'll maybe try sneakin' in close — all sides of us. If the moon's bright, no clouds, we got the edge."

"What d'you suppose they're doin' right now?" asked Mulligan.

"Tendin' their wounded, spellin' their critters," shrugged Jeb. "Just bidin' their time. Corsario'll be plannin' their next move."

"By now, they could be camped in that stand of timber we passed on our way here," Larry thoughtfully suggested.

"Might be," agreed Jeb.

"Why?" challenged Mulligan. "You gettin' notions again?"

"Stockade's high," remarked Larry. "Too high for a rider to reach at a leap. But, if they're countin' on scalin' the walls under cover of dark, they could be cuttin' branches while we're talkin', riggin' ladders."

"Bad cess to 'em all," scowled Mulligan.

"Somethin' to keep in mind," said Larry. "We collected plenty six-shooters out there. Every trooper on guard tonight, might help if he's packin' a handgun along with rifles. Easier to shoot down at marauders tryin' to climb — pistol's better'n a rifle for that kind of action. Every man ought to have a brace of 'em."

"That's somethin' else I'll pass on to Captain Blore," decided Mulligan.

"I'll go talk to him now."

He descended from the parapet and crossed the parade ground to find Blore perched awkwardly on a stool outside the door to his quarters. The captain was smoking a cigar, but didn't seem to be enjoying it.

"Save your breath, Sergeant," was his greeting. "We have two wounded, I know. And at ease for heaven's sake, Mulligan. In our present circumstances, let's not stand on ceremony."

"Yes, Captain," said Mulligan, hunkering, nudging his hat off his forehead. "Well, so you know how it went. We did pretty good. This first attack sure cost Corsario."

"He has more men than he lost."

"That's so, sir."

"Somewhat foolhardy, wasn't it, opening the gates for those adventurers?"

"Valentine's idea. Like you probably know, when he gets a notion, his partner goes along with it. Their idea was to pick up all the arms and ammo they could tote. No guessin' how many

115

attacks there'll be, sir. Extra weapons're gonna be handy."

"Valentine certainly has a point. And how are our non-military allies faring?"

"Jeb's fine. Them drifters ain't bullet-proof, but they got the damnedest luck. A bullet blew Emerson's hat off without burnin' a hair of his head."

Blore nodded moodily and asked, "What is Jeb Penn's assessment of the situation?"

"We're all workin' on hunches," said Mulligan.

"And everybody's guess is . . . ?" prodded Blore.

"It'll be after sundown when they move on us again," said Mulligan. "Sneak attacks, if it's dark enough. Might be somethin' to Valentine's notion they're riggin' ladders in the timber far south. We got extra pistols now. He says every guard ought to be packin' a couple."

"I have to agree," said Blore. "You'll see to it?"

"Leave it to me, sir," urged Mulligan.

"You're in command, but I'm your legs."

Blore winced in exasperation.

"First time for me," he confided. "Until it happens to him, a man just doesn't realize how restricting a broken leg can be. All right, Sergeant, roster the men. They should take turns to rest themselves."

"Take care of that rightaway," said Mulligan, getting to his feet.

He was accosted by Larry when he was halfway across the compound.

"I just thought of . . . " began Larry.

"Got yourself another notion, huh?" challenged Mulligan. "You're doin' fine so far, so let me hear it."

"You'd have a lot of lamps here," said Larry. "Which means you're holdin' a good supply of coal oil."

"Plenty," nodded Mulligan.

"Stored where?" asked Larry.

Mulligan jerked a thumb.

"Shack closest the last well west."

"Fire arrows, Sarge," frowned Larry.

117

"I still got this feelin' they'll try burnin' us out."

"And you could be right," Mulligan conceded.

"So the stuff oughtn't be stored in the one place," declared Larry. "If an arrow, any kind of firebrand, hits that shack, there could be a big blast before anybody gets time to douse it. All that oil. Other places could catch fire, officers' quarters, barracks, stables, even the main block. Might be smart to leave only a couple cans in there, have most of the oil stashed all around, but clear of the fences and any other fire-trap."

"I'm startin' to savvy how you hot shots've survived so long," grinned Mulligan. "Never stop thinkin', do you?"

"That's what a brain's for," said Larry.

"It'll be taken care of," said Mulligan. "Meanwhile, you and your partner ought to get the load off your feet while you can."

He assigned Yarrow and Frost the task of near emptying the fuel shack, then made for the quartermaster's store for a few words with Elvey. His colleague was completing inspection, testing and reloading of the pistols taken from dead bandidos.

"How're those wounded boys makin' out, Emmett?" he asked.

"I'll take a look at 'em next," said Mulligan. "Looks like we got plenty handguns, huh?"

"We weren't short of weapons," said Elvey. "Now we got . . . " He frowned and checked himself. "Hell, I almost said more than we need — as if we can't use every piece of hardware available."

"Two each for the troopers on night guard, Mose," said Mulligan. "If it's gonna be a dark one, if marauders get close to the stockades, they'll do better with pistols, won't have to show as much of 'emselves as when they're aimin' a rifle."

"That makes good sense," approved

119

Elvey. "You're thinkin' of everything, Emmett."

"Comes to brain-work, don't give me all the credit," Mulligan said as he left him.

When he entered the infirmary, Gleddon and O'Curran were in good voice, pointedly excluding the younger soldier from their conversation; they lay on side-by-side cots. Ainsworth was again swabbing the operating table.

"Keep it clean, Major Richards always says," he remarked as Mulligan approached him. "Cuts down on the danger of open wounds becoming infected."

"Gettin' weary, boy?" demanded Mulligan.

"Not yet, Sergeant," said Ainsworth.

"You don't have to stay on your feet every minute," offered Mulligan. "Spell yourself as often as you can. Bound to be more casualties, and you need to stay sharp."

"I do realize that," Ainsworth assured him.

"This is your duty post till the major gets back," Mulligan pointed out. "You're in charge of the infirmary, which means you don't have to take no sass from casualties. These two plug-uglies been givin' you troubles?"

"No, Sergeant," said Ainsworth.

"O'Curran's got plenty to be thankful for?"

"More than he knows. A half inch further left and the bullet would've torn half his face away. All it took was the lobe of his right ear. He'll heal as Gleddon will, given time. And his hearing isn't affected."

"You sure of that?"

"They've been talking ever since Mrs Richards fed them. Gleddon mumbles a lot, but O'Curran catches every word he utters."

"Ever laid out a dead man, kid?" The question was voiced bluntly. Ainsworth shook his head, but didn't flinch. "It might come to that. We stopped a lot of 'em, but we're still outnumbered — heavily."

"I won't enjoy it, but I'll do whatever must be done," promised Ainsworth.

Mulligan collected a chair on his way to the wounded men. He placed it by Gleddon's cot, straddled it and folded his arms on its back, studying both men sternly.

"Trooper Ainsworth tells me you ain't givin' him a hard time," he muttered. "Keep it that way, hear?"

"Oh, he's a real gentle kid that oughtn't be here anyway," sneered O'Curran. "He works best away from the fightin'."

"Good at what he's doin', and don't you forget it," growled Mulligan. "A wounded soldier can only lose so much blood, savvy? Else he's a dead soldier. Wasn't for Ainsworth, you could've bled to death, you too, Gleddon."

"Yeah, well . . . " began the big redhead.

"And another thing," stressed Mulligan. "When a broken bone ain't set right, a casualty's in danger. Ask me what kind of danger and I'll ask you — ever hear of gangrene? You won't lose that arm, Gleddon, and Captain Blore won't end up one-legged, because the kid works good, because he heeded everything the regimental surgeon's taught him." He rose and nudged the chair aside. "Keep that in mind, okay?"

He left the infirmary. From the south parapet, Jake Ulric signalled him; all quiet on the flats surrounding the fort. Now he could begin rostering the defenders to get some rest, half of them relaxing, the others standing guard.

When Larry returned to the section of catwalk left of the gateway, Jeb was squatting crosslegged, hat tipped over his eyes, rifle resting on his knees, his back resting against the timbers of the stockade. He was dozing. Larry pantomimed for Stretch to do likewise, then positioned himself facing southward and rolled and lit a cigarette. How long before the next assault? He clung to his hunch. Something sneaky next time. And tonight for sure. Maybe early. Maybe midnight or later.

The women of Fort Mitchum cooked and served lunch. The hot afternoon dragged on to the cool of evening, at which time the women reappeared. Supper for the defenders was beef stew and plenty of it. Mesdames Harrington and Toone had been baking; apple pie to follow the stew, then as much coffee as the men wanted.

It began after everybody had eaten. The wind blew from the south, so the men guarding that side of the fort were first to hear it. Faint, but audible, relentless, monotonous. The enemy serenading them? It didn't sound that way to Larry and Stretch. More like a dirge.

"What d'you make of it, Jeb?" drawled Stretch. "Ever hear it before?"

The old scout spat in disgust while filling and lighting his corncob pipe.

"Death chant," he said. "Yup, I've heard it before. That fat sonofabitch Henriquez — his greasers're doin' most

124

of the singin', but with plenty Injuns join in."

"What is that — Spanish?" Pike Yarrow called to them from the right side of the gateway.

"Bastard Spanish, kinda," was Jeb's reply. "South of the Bravo, I've heard 'em sing it at funerals. Henriquez's bandidos made up their own words sounds like."

Larry glanced over his shoulder. Several women had emerged from the main building; they too were listening. But, though that porch was a considerable distance from the south wall, he made a mental bet they were more inquisitive than alarmed.

"You savvy any of it?" he asked.

The old scout puffed on his pipe, squinted and listened intently, then quoted a few lines.

"We are many — you are few. Them that stand against us're doomed. Death will come to you." He shrugged impatiently. "And stuff like that. A mess o' hogwash. They mean to spook us. Old Comanchero trick. Hell, they might's well whistle in the dark. They got more to fear'n us."

"I've heard sweeter singin' in whorehouses," Yarrow said derisively.

"Comes to music, I ain't no expert," remarked Stretch. "But I got ten bucks in my boot says half of 'em're out of tune."

"No bet," Larry said with a mirthless grin. His grin faded as he raised his eyes to the night sky. "Damn and blast."

"Somethin' fazin' you?" prodded Jeb.

"Give me a choice, I'll settle for one or the other," scowled Larry. "Pitch dark or bright moonlight. Not *this* kind of sky. Look up there."

Jeb and Stretch stared upward.

"Uh huh," grunted Stretch. "Moon's plumb bright, but I see many a cloudbank. Well, we savvy what *that* means."

"Means we'll get both — 'stead of one or the other," grouched Larry. "Plenty light near bright as day for a while, then clouds'll hide the moon and it'll be black as a cardsharp's heart out there."

"Right," nodded Jeb. "And, if it stays dark long enough, marauders could close in from all around us. Won't be mounted this time. They'll come afoot — less chance we'll hear 'em."

"I don't have to pass the word," Larry decided after spotting Mulligan on the east catwalk. "He savvies what could happen. It's for sure he's alertin' the troops."

Mulligan came to them a few minutes later.

"Lousy singin'," he commented, frowning southward. "Not a good Irish tenor in the whole stinkin' pack of 'em. And too much cloud up there for my likin'."

"That's what I've been sayin'," muttered Larry.

"We could have full dark any time," said Mulligan. "So I called every man out. Got Sykes and Janney on the east side, and Frost watchin' north. I'll take the west side with Yarrow. Jeb, you stay put. Mose and Jake'll stay on the other side of the gate and . . . " He touched the trouble-shooters, "you two better patrol all around, put yourselves wherever you're needed. I guess we all know what to look out for?"

"Damn right," growled Jeb. "And we better be sharp-eared. They try sneakin' in on us, we'll hear 'em 'fore we see 'em."

"Watch the flats," Mulligan cautioned as he moved away. "And the sky. Watch the sky."

In the parlor of the commanding officer's quarters, Mattie Delmer plied her needle, serenely working on her embroidery and hoping her demeanor would rub off on the other women.

"We need be in no doubt as to John's reaction to what he finds at Rowansburg, my dears, and the decision he'll at once make. He'll be furious of course, but he won't waste time ranting. There'll be an immediate turnaround. The Eighth will return to base with all speed."

"They'll be here in time to save the fort, I'm sure of that," Sarah said calmly.

"We can hold out till then," declared Beth Richards.

"And we're amply provisioned here," said Polly Glynn. "Nobody will go hungry, the children, the men, any of us." She winced and glanced to a window. "That monotonous singing."

Sarah aired her knowledge.

"Old Comanchero ruse — and so obvious," she shrugged. "Calculated to demoralize us, but boring really."

"I guess, as they're so far from the fort, it's not loud enough to disturb the children's sleep," murmured Naomi.

"The children." Polly Glynn sighed sentimentally. "So obedient, so easy to control at this time, much as though they realize this is what we most need of them."

"We should never underestimate the instincts of the very young," smiled Mattie.

"That first attack — so violent," frowned Elmira Landis. "It's a mercy, near miraculous, that only two troopers were wounded. They'll recover, Beth?"

"If they accept that they're medically unfit for duty," said the surgeon's wife.

"Being difficult, are they?" asked Mattie.

"Troopers Gleddon and O'Curran always have been," said Beth. "Bellicose by nature, Mattie. When the next attack comes, George's protege, young Ainsworth, may have to secure them to their cots. They'll be that eager to get into the fighting."

On the east catwalk, Sykes and Janney scanned the sky, noted the cloudbank rolling toward the moon and promptly stubbed out their cigars.

"Too many Injuns backin' Corsario," scowled Janney.

"Get mad and stay mad, Biff," advised Sykes. "The madder you get, the harder you fight."

"They like the dark," muttered

Janney. "Gives 'em a chance to close in on us — hell take 'em."

"Let 'em try," said Sykes. "We'll be ready for 'em. Won't spot 'em till they're *real* close, but that's fine by me. We got pistols now. At close range, we'll stop the sonsabitches."

With the moon obscured, the defenders could no longer see clear across the flats. In a matter of minutes, the darkness was intense. On the west side with Yarrow, Mulligan didn't even think of calling for extra vigilance. Such a warning would have been unnecessary.

"Feelin' in your bones?" Stretch quietly challenged his partner.

"We'll be havin' uninvited company," predicted Larry. "Any time from now on."

On the north catwalk, a little after midnight, Curly Frost cocked an ear, also a pistol.

5

Moonlight and Mayhem

THE sound was barely audible but, like every other guard, Frost's ears were attuned to the night sounds, the predictable and the familiar, such as the distant wail of a coyote or the cry of a bird. And the not so familiar sounds, anything closer at hand.

What he heard was wood against wood less than two yards from where he stood. Quietly, he moved those two yards and thrust his head over the parapet, his eyes probing the gloom below.

A pole, a branch trimmed of its foliage, had been positioned against the outside of the stockade. He saw the climbing Comanche making his ascent stealthily, using left hand and bare knees, a lance at the ready in his free hand. He saw the Comanche at the moment the Comanche saw him and had the presence of mind to sidestep to his right before squeezing trigger. The lance hurtled through the space between his head and his left shoulder as the Colt roared.

With the echo of the shot, the marauder fell backward. Frost promptly reached over and down to grasp the pole left-handed, intending to haul it up before a second Comanche could begin climbing. He couldn't budge it. Too heavy, which meant a second redman was already shinning up it. He recocked, aimed downward, fired again, heard a scream of agony and tried pulling on the pole again. This time he managed it. Hastily, he hauled it up and tossed it into the compound. It thudded to the dust a few feet from where the lance had embedded.

The two gunshots were more than enough warming for the other guards.

"You okay, Frost?" bellowed Mulligan.

"Still here!" came Frost's reply. "Stopped a couple tryin' to come over the wall!"

"Stay sharp, everybody!" cautioned Mulligan.

A head appeared above the east side of the stockade, then a hand brandishing a tomahawk. Biff Janney was close, almost at arm's length, and gave the marauder no chance to use the tomahawk, thrust a six-gun almost into the Comanche's face and discharged it. The Comanche dropped from view. Sykes leaned forward, darted a glance downward and swore luridly.

"A ladder! Hell!"

"Pull it up," urged Janney. "I'll give you cover."

Using both hands, Sykes began hauling the makeshift ladder up and over. Down below, a musket barked. The ball missed the trooper's head by less than an inch and, while he kept on hauling, Janney aimed for the flash of the weapon, fired again and heard a howl of pain.

The ladder was drawn up and dropped from the catwalk while, on the south side, a thudding sound alerted the trouble-shooters.

"Knockin' 'em off the ladders is only half the job," Larry said grimly, hefting his Colt. "We got to pull 'em up so no others can climb 'em."

The thudding sound compelled them to raise themselves and peer downward. The climbers were barely visible and only the top of the ladder.

"Get 'em off of there," urged Stretch, reaching down to grasp the top rung.

A hurled tomahawk skimmed the top of Larry's Stetson in the instant before his Colt boomed twice. He scored on both marauders, after which Stretch heaved. The ladder, improvised of sapling rods and twine, started upward. He got his other hand to it and, moments later, it was tumbling into the compound. Then he ducked hastily and a lance cut through air where his head and shoulders had been an instant before.

Larry threw himself sideways and checked its flight. Left-handed, he caught the missile and reversed it. Holstering his Colt, he muttered to Stretch.

"Take a quick look. Any more comin' up?"

Stretch raised himself, ducked again and growled, "About three yards to your left."

Pacing that distance away from his partner, Larry thrust his head over the stockade. Directly below, another ladder, three half-naked men scaling it. He slid the lance over, lowered its point and jabbed hard, and suddenly the moon shone again. He saw his victim pitch sideways off the ladder with his throat bloody. Again he thrust downward — harder. The second brave, his face contorted, grasped at the shaft of the lance with its point buried in his chest. Larry let go and, as that one began falling, the third climber made to leap clear, but not fast enough; Stretch shot him twice.

On the other side of the gate, Elvey blew invaders off two ladders with a shotgun. Ulric immediately hauled up and discarded the ladders.

Thanks to the moonlight, Mulligan, Yarrow and the drifters had clear targets, more Comanches rushing the east wall, preparing to set ladders against it. With pistol fire, they downed eight would-be climbers.

From his part of the south wall, Jebb Penn got a Winchester working to deadly effect, accounting for five more.

Stretch raised his voice above the racket of gunfire. He had to, to make himself heard by the guard at the north side.

"Need any help back there?"

"They keep comin'!" was Frost's yelled complaint.

Taking up a Winchester, Stretch bounded past Mulligan and Yarrow, on to the northeast corner, then along to where Frost was ducking to avoid death from three airborne lances.

"C'mon, amigo," he said encouragingly. "While the moonlight holds — give 'em hell."

They rose up after Frost grabbed a fully loaded Winchester and, together, raked advancing redmen with rapid fire. Five lurched and went down; the others scattered.

"Trooper Frost?" called Mulligan.

"They're vamoosin' this side," answered Frost.

"This side too," yelled Mulligan. "Janney — Sykes?"

"They won't be back till dark!" roared Janney.

"Retreatin' from this side too!" boomed Ulric.

"Cease fire!" ordered Mulligan.

As the din subsided, the brainwave hit Larry like a physical blow. He raised his eyes to the sky as Stretch came hurrying back to him.

"Big cloudbank on the way," he observed. "But, it we move fast enough — we'll maybe have just time enough."

"To do what?" demanded Stretch.

138

"To rig a bad surprise for 'em, give us clear targets when the moonlight quits on us again," said Larry. "This time, they don't have to open the gates for us."

He confided his plan as he and Stretch descended to the compound, then called to Elvey. The quartermaster sergeant listened to his instructions and hesitated, but only for a moment.

"Do it, Mose!" urged Mulligan. "Any trick Valentine thinks of is fine by me!"

Elvey followed the drifters down to the compound and hurried on to be lost from sight a while. The tall men were collecting ladders, lances and poles and throwing them up to the catwalks. Working against time, Larry darting glances skyward, they returned to the catwalks and began hurling the ladders and missiles with all their might, and with accuracy.

"Little heaps yonder of every side of the stockade — anything that'll burn," panted Stretch; "You get the damnedest notions, runt."

"Full dark gives 'em an edge," muttered Larry. "The hell with 'em. *We* need an edge!"

Sighting Blore balanced on his crutch in the doorway to his quarters, Mulligan made a hasty descent and ran to him.

"Situation under control, sir. Best you get back inside, leave everything to . . . "

"Tell me what's happening," ordered Blore. "And — where is Sergeant Elvey taking those cans of oil . . . ?"

"We figure they'll try for the walls again when the moonlight fails us," Mulligan quickly explained. "They must've rigged ladders in the timber south, sir. As well as fightin' 'em off, we've been pullin' the ladders over the walls . . . "

"To prevent other marauders using them, yes, I understand that," nodded Blore. "But now those drifters are throwing the ladders out again."

"They know where they're throwin' that stuff, the ladders, the lances,"

Mulligan assured him. "We're makin' piles outside the stockade, but far enough away so the stockade won't catch fire."

"Won't — what . . . ?"

"That's what the oil's for. We'll dump a can with the stopper loosened on every heap. When it's dark again, we'll give the enemy time to come sneakin' back, then throw fire-brands on them heaps. Light, Captain! The heaps blazin' all sides of the fort! We'll be pickin' the spalpeens off before they can get inside thirty feet of the stockade walls!"

"By Judas!"

"Helluva notion, sir. It could work."

"Any more of our men out of action?"

"No, sir. Some close calls, but . . . "

"Then get to it. Help Valentine and his friend every way you can!"

When debris of the first night attack had been hurled beyond all four walls, Larry checked the sky again and hustled along the catwalks, noting the location of each pile. Not big piles, as he remarked to Elvey, but sufficient for their purpose.

"Trouble is," warned Elvey. "If we try to hurl the cans that far, we could miss our mark."

"You got the firebrands ready?" asked Larry.

"Four," nodded Elvey. "Throwin' them'll be easy enough, but I don't know about those cans."

Larry now had second thoughts about their ability to set their flares from atop the stockade. He called to the men on the south side after another glance upward.

"No sign of 'em?"

"Nothin'!" came the old scout's reply.

"All right, let me have them cans," urged Larry. "Ought to be just time enough to dump 'em where we want 'em. Have the guards open the gates a mite."

He called to Stretch and, moments later, with the moonlight again fading, they moved through a small opening in the gates toting two cans apiece. Larry doused the piles at the south and east sides, leaving the cans atop them, their stoppers loosened. Stretch repeated this process, running to the piles west and north, then hustling around front to rejoin his partner. It was pitch dark again when they re-entered the fort; the guard secured the gates.

The catwalks were manned again in expectation of further attempts to climb the walls. An oil-soaked firebrand was in readiness on the east rampart, where Mulligan and Yarrow looked to their weapons. Another within reach of the drifters and Jeb, the third hefted by Janney on the west side, the fourth with Frost on the north side, now partnered by Ulric.

"We didn't hear nothin' last time," Janney muttered to Sykes. "Ain't likely we'll hear nothin' this time neither."

"We better hear *somethin'*," fretted Sykes. "Be a powerful shame — us wastin' all that oil."

"The saddlebum that put Red on his back, he gets the damnedest ideas," mused Janney.

"Mighty cunnin' feller," agreed Sykes.

"I guess that's what we need here," decided Janney. "Corsario's a sly bastard, him and all his bunch. We're just gonna have to be some smarter'n 'em, if we hope to be still breathin' when the rest of the outfit comes home."

On the north catwalk, Frost raised his eyes and winced.

"Will you look at that consarn cloudbank?" he sourly invited. "Big'un, Sarge. And it don't look like it's movin'."

"It'll be coal-black out there for an hour or more," Ulric calculated. "No use us talkin' about it. Better we stay quiet — and listen."

The tall men nursed cocked rifles on the catwalk left of the gates, flanking Jeb and probing the gloom.

"Smell 'em, Jeb?" asked Stretch.

"Not yet," said Jeb. "But I figure

they'll come a'sneakin' purty soon. And the hell of it is they can see in the dark, them Comanches anyway."

Ten minutes later, out of patience and craving action, Larry insisted, "We might's well find out one way or the other. Stretch, let's see if they can spot your hat."

"Why *my* hat?" demanded Stretch. "You could as easy poke yours up."

"You already got a hole in yours," Larry pointed out.

"Ain't that the truth," grouched Stretch.

He bared his head, reversed a rifle, set his Stetson atop the stock and slowly raised it some twelve inches above the stockade. If there were marauders out there, could any of them spot this inviting target in the dark?

One did. Somewhere south, a musket barked and, for the second time since the battle of Fort Mitchum began, the taller trouble-shooter's hat was holed and sent spinning across the area north of the gates. He swore explosively.

"So we know they're closin' in," growled Larry. He raised his voice and his lusty baritone was heard by the other defenders. "Firebrands — *now!*"

He scratched a match, held it to the end of a brand, drew his arm back and hurled it with unerring accuracy. It landed atop a heap of oil-soaked ladders, which at once flared. The coal oil can exploded and a wide area of the flats south was caught in the sudden glow.

Janney, Ulric and then Mulligan lit and threw their brands just as accurately with the same result. The piles flared on all sides of the stockade, suddenly illuminating the area, revealing two score or more marauders closing in, toting makeshift ladders, poles, ropes — and weapons which they hastily readied for action.

"Let 'em have it!" yelled Mulligan.

Rifles barked in rapid fire from the catwalks. Scattering hostiles retaliated, the redmen loosing arrows and hurling lances, the Mexicans cutting loose with six-guns, until the defenders began scoring and cries of agony rose high above the racket of gunfire. Caught in the hail of bullets, marauders reeled, staggering, lurching, many of them pitching to the dust at the moment of the impact of hot lead. Jeb and the tall men discarded empty rifles, reached for replacements and kept up the onslaught on raiders visible from the south wall, making every shot count.

On the north side, a fleeing Mexican's feet became entangled in a ladder half-dropped by a mortally wounded Comanche. As he struggled to free himself, he howled from the searing agony of rifle-slugs mercilessly triggered by Frost and Sergeant Ulric.

Death came close to Sykes and Janney, but not close enough. They ducked as arrows and hurled tomahawks and lances sped their way, then rose with their rifles clattering in angry challenge, triggering fast but accurately. In the glow of the fire beyond the west fence, they saw one of Henriquez's bandidos pawing at his chest and flopping to his knees. Another died on his feet, his face bloody. A Comanche, his shoulder creased, over-balanced, spun and fell screaming into the blazing heap.

From their vantage-point, Mulligan and Yarrow made small targets of themselves and kept their rifles working. No ladder-carriers got within twenty yards of the stockade. They were the first to die. Relentlessly, Mulligan and the trooper then directed fire at marauders beginning a ragged retreat.

"Sonofabitch!" exclaimed Jeb.

"You hit?" demanded Larry.

"Can't you blame well smell my hair?" scowled Jeb. "Pour water on me, for pity's sakes! I'm afire!"

"No you ain't neither," grinned Stretch.

"I smell it good, but you ain't burnin', ain't even smoking," Larry observed. "Slug must've cut through just where your hair dangles at your shoulders. Close one, amigo. You must live right."

He cursed as an arrow sped past his face, took sight on the bowman silhouetted against the firelight and put a bullet in his chest. Simultaneously, Stretch scored on a running bandido.

In the infirmary, Ainsworth was having trouble with his patients. Gleddon and O'Curran were on their feet and abusing him; he had locked the door and stood with his back to it.

"We gotta get out there, Ainsworth!" raged O'Curran. "Stand aside, damn you!"

"It's still too soon for you two," insisted Ainsworth. "Take my word, if you tried climbing to a catwalk, you'd never make it. You'd probably collapse half-way across the compound."

"We're strong enough to . . . !" began Gleddon.

"You aren't strong enough yet," retorted Ainsworth. "Argue with me tomorrow, not tonight. You don't realize just how much blood you've lost. Until you've compensated for that loss, you *can't* get into action. Your strength would fail you. The weakness would affect your eyesight. You'd move too slowly."

"Nothin' wrong with my eyes," scowled the big redhead. "I could see you clear enough, Ainsworth, if you'd *quit swayin'*! Why the hell're you doin' that? Stand still!"

"I haven't moved an inch since you got to your feet," declared Ainsworth. "Haven't budged, and that's the truth. *Now* will you believe me?"

"Hell's sakes," groaned O'Curran, lurching back to his cot, flopping. "It's crazy. How much can a man bleed from a little nick in his damn ear?"

"As much as Gleddon bled from that wound in his side," Ainsworth said grimly. "No matter what you men think of me, heed what I'm telling you for your own sake. If you won't believe me, believe Major Richards. He's told me of soldiers in combat bleeding to death from scalp wounds, a bullet-gashed hand, a perforated foot."

"Us and our stinkin' luck," complained Gleddon.

"You both managed to cross the compound and reach the infirmary," said Ainsworth. "That was quite an achievement, quite a feat of strength. You made it, but a lot of your blood soaked into the ground between."

Polly Glynn and Naomi Landis had heard sounds softer than the wails of mortally wounded raiders, despite the clamor of shooting. Or maybe they hadn't, maybe it was feminine instinct that drew them to Barracks 4 to light lamps and check on the children. Their sleep broken by the uproar, some were sitting up in their cots.

The younger boys, gruffly reprimanded by George Richards Junior, stayed quiet. Two little girls were weeping in fear. The women hurried to them.

"Hush, Emma dear," soothed Polly, embracing one of them. "Don't be afraid of the noise. You're safe here."

Naomi perched on the other cot and

held hands with a sobbing moppet.

"Nothing to worry about, Lucille," she murmured. "Nothing at all. Those are mostly Fort Mitchum guns you're hearing. Brave soldiers will make the bad men go away, I promise you." She wiped away tears and dabbed at a button nose with the hem of her gown. "Your daddy will be coming home. It won't be long before you're sitting on his knee again. You'll like that, won't you? And I want to tell him what a brave little girl you've been, but you wouldn't want me to lie to him, would you?" The child shook her head. "That's right, Lucille. Stop crying."

"Can you stay with me?" the little girl begged.

"For as long as you want," smiled Naomi, gathering her into her arms. "You know, it seems only yesterday I was as little as you."

"Tell me a story," the other child begged Polly.

"A story about me?" suggested Polly. "All right, here we go. Once upon a time, there was a little girl — exactly like you — and her name was Polly McKinley, and she thought horse soldiers were the most wonderful men in the world. She kept telling her mother how, when she grew up, she wanted to be a cavalryman's wife. Well, as time passed . . . "

In their night attire, the other women were gathered by the barricaded door of the administration block, listening to the barking of rifles and the booming of six-shooters.

"I should be on one of those catwalks," Sarah Delmer said irritably.

"Mattie, if you won't say it, I will — though you outrank me," frowned Elmira Landis. "Sarah, don't talk nonsense."

"I outrank you, you say, Ellie," smiled the colonel's wife. "Listen to us, the so-called weaker sex, automatically assuming the authority of our husbands. Don't worry, Ellie. Sarah will obey the orders of the officer in command."

"Captain Blore is hardly in a condition

to . . . " began Sarah. Feeling Marj Blore's eyes on her, she bit her lip. "No offence, but you must admit he's not at his best."

"I think the crutch irritates him almost as much as having a leg in splints," said Marj. "But his mind isn't affected. Not for a moment does he forget he's still in charge. Sergeant Mulligan briefs him all the time, and our defenders, including non-military personnel, are using tactics of which he approves."

"We are bound by the captain's instructions as relayed to us by Marj," Mattie reminded her daughter. "We have weapons, but we're to use them only as a last resort. Until — I should say *if* — the raiders scale the stockade, we must remain indoors, defending ourselves from barricaded windows." She nodded to Marj. "A logical command, Marj. I'm sure John would approve. It would be his wish as well."

"Am I indulging in wishful thinking, or am I hearing less shooting now?"

frowned Leona Harrington.

"It does seem to be becoming less noisy out there," said Beth Richards.

A few minutes later, the defenders heard Mulligan's bawled command.

"Hold your fire!"

The men listened intently while reloading weapons. Slowly, the fires were dying, but the moon shone again; they could see for a considerable distance beyond the area strewn with the corpses of redskins and bandidos. The survivors of the second assault force were disappearing to the south and well out of range now.

"They've vamoosed again, Emmett!" announced Jeb.

"Anybody bleedin'?" demanded Elvey.

"Check for wounded!" ordered Mulligan. "I oughtn't need a roll call! Just look around!"

Silence for a few moments. Then Biff Janney yelled from the west catwalk.

"I can scarce believe it, but we're still here."

"Any man hurtin', name yourself!" urged Mulligan.

"I got a bunion's givin' me hell!" Sykes facetiously complained.

Ulric guffawed. Yarrow whooped and slapped his knee. Larry and Stretch traded grins with Jeb and began chuckling.

"Reload!" Mulligan's voice again. "Half of you rest — smoke if you want! The other half watch them stiffs careful 'case some of 'em ain't as dead as they look!"

He descended from the east catwalk. Trudging across the compound, he saw the captain balanced on his crutch by a well, lighting a cigar. He confronted Blore and saluted respectfully.

"At ease, Sergeant," frowned Blore. "Report."

"We're still holdin' 'em off, sir. Third attack failed. And it cost Corsario a lot more men."

"We have no more wounded?"

"Luck of the Irish, sir. And our stockade was built to last."

"We aren't all Irish, Sergeant, but I'm sure you'll claim your Irish luck's rubbing off on all of us."

"There's enough of it to go around, sir. Did you know Valentine and Emerson're of Irish ancestry? Texas-born, but . . ."

"Enough of your bragging, you whimsical Mick," Blore good-humoredly chided. "I think I should address the men. Kindly announce me, and accompany me to the centre of the parade ground — in case this damn-blasted crutch fails me and put me flat on my face."

"This way, sir," offered Mulligan.

"I do know where the half-way mark is," said Blore.

"Yessir," grinned Mulligan.

"This'll be informal," Blore said as they moved off. "Don't call them to attention. Just announce me and assure them it won't be a long speech."

When they reached the flagpole dead centre of the compound, Mulligan called to the men on the catwalks.

"Stay at ease! Captain Blore's got somethin' to say, so every man listen up, okay?" He nodded to Blore. "They're waitin', sir."

"Can you all hear me — or do I have to bellow at you as the sergeant does?" demanded Blore.

"Hearin' you clear, Cap'n," replied Janney.

"As you know, until the regiment returns, I'm the officer in command," said Blore. "So now, as your temporary commandant, I commend you for your efforts, your courage and your devotion to duty. We are a pitifully small force, a mere handful compared to those fanatical Comancheros, but we are holding out and will continue to hold out until the main body of the Eighth appears on the north horizon . . . " He raised his voice. "When Colonel Delmer will order a charge and decimate the enemy — and that's for damn sure!"

Stretch's applause was a rebel yell. Jerry Sykes cheered, laughed and declared, "You're tellin' it true, Cap'n!"

"Button your lip, Sykes!" ordered Mulligan. "Let the captain finish!"

"I'm sure I speak for the colonel's wife and all the ladies and children of Fort Mitchum," Blore continued. "You have earned their gratitude and admiration by your gallant resistance against a superior force — superior in numbers, but not in fighting spirit. Soldiers of the Eighth, my respects. Jebediah, old friend, what can I say? When this regiment needed you, you were always with us. Mister Valentine, Mister Emerson . . . " Good psychology, his decision to end his address in jocular vein. "With you on our side, how in blazes did the South manage to lose the Civil War?"

"Well, hell," replied Larry. "*We* didn't want to quit fightin'. It was all *their* idea. I'm pretty sure Lee and Grant cut cards to decide who'd surrender to who."

Blore waited for the laughter to subside, then said fervently, "Stand firm against the enemy, be of good heart and, with God's help, we'll hold out for as long as we have to!"

The men cheered him as he turned and, still using his crutch awkwardly, returned to his quarters.

Marj awaited him there. She smiled wistfully and kissed him.

"That signifies approval of my little speech," he assumed.

"You were wonderful," she declared. "*They're* wonderful, and they believed every word you said to them."

"You too, I hope?" he challenged.

"Don't worry about me or any of the other women," she said. "We truly believe, Tom. We'll survive and so will Fort Mitchum, because the regiment will return in time."

"Time is the vital factor," he muttered, lowering himself to a chair. "Time and distance, the speed with which the Eighth can make the journey home. But I'm confident, Marj. The colonel's a wily old veteran. He'll bring them home well-mounted, the horses strong

160

enough for the charge. He's too shrewd to order a fast run all the way south from Rowansburg. There'll be rest stops to spell horses and men. That's the way it has to be."

The drifters talked quietly out of deference to Jeb Penn, now huddled on his side against the stockade, sleeping the sleep of utter exhaustion, snoring steadily.

"Got ourselves in a rough one this time," remarked Stretch.

"Better we think of what we got goin' for us," said Larry, stifling a yawn. "U.S. Army builds strong forts. Ain't a bullet could cut through this stockade and, when we got to fight off a charge, we got plenty cover. Grub ain't short nor ammunition. The women and kids're stayin' steady . . . "

"Sure," nodded Stretch.

" . . . and they've come at us three times and took a lickin'," Larry continued. "Only two of us wounded, but Corsario's lost a helluva lot of men already — so we're doin' fine."

"Hey, I ain't complainin', ain't nervous neither," Stretch gently assured him.

"You're right anyway," conceded Larry. "This's a rough one. And the biggest ruckus we've mixed into in a month of Sundays."

"I'm just remarkin' it ain't over yet," said Stretch. "We killed a lot of Comancheros, but they still got us outnumbered." He paused a moment, then said offhandedly, "Could be our last ruckus, runt."

"Could be," Larry had to acknowledge. "Then again, it depends, you know? The other soldierboys, whole damn outfit, might come poundin' back hell for leather when we most need 'em. Then it'll be finished." He added, "Maybe *we'll* be finished by then. On the other hand, maybe we'll still be on our feet and shootin' raiders."

"We'll find out," drawled Stretch.

"Uh huh," grunted Larry. "We'll find out — one way or the other."

At sunrise, when the women began busying themselves, fixing breakfast, the flats surrounding Fort Mitchum were devoid of any sign of life. A lot of Comancheros out there, but horizontal, sprawled, huddled, twisted in the grotesque postures of sudden death.

Upon waking, Jeb soberly warned all in earshot of him, "We been whittlin' 'em down purty good, but they ain't through with us yet. For all we know, since the last sneak-raid, could be a hundred more Injuns joined up with Corsario south of here. So don't nobody start cheerin' yet."

Food had never tasted so good. When the women emerged to carry laden trays up to the catwalks, the defenders caught the aroma of bacon, eggs, hot biscuits and coffee. Their mouths watered.

While they were climbing the steps, Larry called to them all, "Thanks for the chow, ladies, but don't linger to socialize, okay? And don't peek over the parapets. You don't need to see what's out there."

Moments later, Sarah Delmer was presenting him with a filled platter. He accepted it and muttered his thanks and then, after matching stares with him, she deliberately moved past him to grasp two top-pointed timbers of the stockade, raise herself and scan the scene of carnage.

Lowering herself, she eyed him again and said casually, "They're *good* Comancheros now."

He watched her move away, thinking, "Lieutenant Grescoe, she's all yours. And better you than me."

While eating, he kept his gaze on the territory south.

6

The Volunteer

AT 8 p.m. of the night of the second assault on Fort Mitchum, Colonel Delmer's regiment was camped by Arroyo Sibora, a tributary of the Pecos. Sun-up tomorrow, they would press northward on the last leg of the relief advance on the great basin and the township dead centre of its verdant floor. But, thanks to the stiff pace they had maintained, horses and men were now exhausted. Every officer, NCO and trooper was eager to be on the move again, but to engage Corsario's force on spent mounts could prove disastrous.

Delmer was in his tent, conferring with his aide-de-camp, Major Landis, and Captains Glynn and Harrington. They studied a map, marked the location of their overnight camp and estimated the distance separating them from their destination.

After several minutes of calculation, Landis said, "Noon, Colonel. Regardless of how early a start we make, that's as soon as we could hope to see Rowansburg."

"I agree," said Harrington.

"Were we to advance from here at the gallop, our animals would be badly winded by the time we attack," opined Glynn. "Colonel?"

"My estimate also," Delmer said morosely. "Damn! It had to be Rowansburg that blasted savage laid siege to. If he'd struck at Bosely to the west or Taegler City to the west, we could've engaged his force less than twelve hours from the time we rode out of Mitchum."

The junior officer who, for the past ten minutes, had eavesdropped outside the commanding officer's tent was Lieutenant Mathew Grescoe, fiance of the colonel's daughter. Before presenting himself, he took a moment to flick dust from his tunic. Six feet tall and of superior education, he had been described by Sarah, also his future mother-in-law, as classically handsome, and this was no exaggeration.

It was well known that he was an ambitious officer eager for promotion. Indeed, his record was envied by some of his seniors.

Thrusting the flap aside, he entered, stood to attention and saluted smartly.

"Permission to interrupt, sir," he requested, "to offer a suggestion and to volunteer."

"At ease, Lieutenant, and permission granted." Delmer worked his cigar to the side of his mouth while the other officers smiled genially; Grescoe was popular. "You wish to volunteer you say? Just what do you have in mind?"

"Advance intelligence, sir," said Grescoe. "If I may consult the map?"

"I'll save you the trouble," said Delmer. "We have estimated the regiment will reach Rowansburg and engage the enemy at noon tomorrow."

"I'm still volunteering, sir," said Grescoe. "If I leave within the hour, I believe I'll see the basin by sunrise. I have field glasses. From a safe distance and out of sight of the Comancheros, I believe I can assess the situation, ascertain if the town is surrounded and the enemy attacking at long range — or already descending the slopes. I could also calculate the enemy's strength."

"And then what?" demanded Delmer.

"Turn south again," said Grescoe. "You'll be en route when I rejoin you and I believe the information I obtain will be of positive value in the planning of your strategy."

"In plain language, we'll know the situation, know what to expect," Landis remarked to the colonel.

"Lieutenant, to do what you're volunteering to do, you'd need to be well mounted," argued Delmer. "Every animal of the regiment was in a condition of exhaustion when we camped here. Animals *and* men, so much so that sentries will be standing only one-hour guards — that being as long as we could expect them to stay on their feet."

"And you may observe I'm having trouble keeping my eyes open," sighed Glynn. "Should I apologize, Colonel?"

"No apology necessary, Captain," winced Delmer, "since I find myself to be in the same sorry state. So, young man, how can you hope to do as you propose?"

"Now *there*'s a question," remarked Landis, "Surely you're as weary as the rest of us, Lieutenant?"

"I don't mean to brag," said Grescoe. "But I have this ability to catnap on a long and slow ride, and manage to stay mounted. I had a good supper and feel equal to the journey to Rowansburg."

"On a winded horse?" frowned Delmer.

"Corporal McBean is inspecting mounts at this moment, sir," said Grescoe. "I took the liberty of assigning him that duty which I'm sure he'll perform thoroughly. He can be relied upon to select a strong horse with a good turn of speed, one that's sufficiently rested."

"Anticipating I'd accede to your request," Delmer said with a knowing grin.

"Of all the intelligence I'll obtain, I believe Corsario's strength would be the most vital," declared Grescoe. "You could then decide . . . "

"Precisely," nodded Delmer. "How best to deploy the regiment in order to cut off the enemy's retreat."

"I would travel light, sir," Grescoe assured him. "It's entirely possible you'll see me within an hour of your beginning the advance on Rowansburg. In dawn's first light, such a reconnaissance should take less than fifteen minutes."

Delmer gave the suggestion some thought, all the time fighting back the impulse to yawn, the other officers eyeing him expectantly, Grescoe hopefully.

"Very well," he said. "Permission granted, Lieutenant. Learn what you can, but proceed with caution."

"Thank you, sir."

Grescoe came to attention, saluted and hurried out. A few minutes later, he was walking the lines to which the cavalry mounts were tied and approaching the tobacco-chewing Corporal McBean.

"How much longer?" he demanded.

"Done made up my mind, Lieutenant," drawled McBean. "This way." He led Grescoe to a rangy black wearing his own saddle. "Checked his wind, checked him all over. This critter's had as much spellin' as the others. Mind now, he ain't ready for a fast run, but give him time, ride him a couple miles easy, spell him another ten minutes and, when you straddle him again, he'll take you where you're headed at a good clip."

"Good work, McBean," grinned Grescoe. "You know horses as well as you know your own parents."

"Better," McBean said dryly. "I *never* knew *them*."

Grescoe swung astride, wheeled the black and started northward at any easy pace, keeping the expert's advice in mind. His mission decided, he could now let his mind drift back to headquarters, specifically to all his memories of the woman to whom he was betrothed.

Wonderful woman, Sarah, proud and beautiful. He counted himself a lucky man, though he had duly noted characteristics he would have to counter after she became his wife. Hints of a mean streak sometimes, a tendency to hauteur, certainly a strong will. He approved of strong-willed women; no officer should take a too-placid woman for his wife. Ladies of the regiment needed strength of character, and hers was as strong as her mother's. But her cool disdain for NCOs and especially the troopers of the Eighth disquieted him. Better she should learn from her mother, whose intelligence he so respected. Mattie Delmer knew how to address troopers in a manner befitting her status as the colonel's lady. But, when spoken to by her, no horse soldier was made to feel like an underling, the lowest of the low; his self respect was left intact.

"You could learn much from your mother, sweetheart," he reflected. "And, after I place that gold band on your elegant finger, there'll be a great deal *I'll* have to teach you. I'll count it an honor to become your husband — but never your whipping boy, never your slave."

By midnight, he was covering the trail to the basin at a gallop, the black serving him well. He kept his patience in check, wisely spelling the animal at intervals.

During one of these pauses, hunkered by his mount on the south side of a seventy-foot high rockmound, he scratched a match, letting it glow just long enough for him to consult his watch. 3.45 a.m. and all quiet. *Too* quiet? By now, shouldn't he be hearing at least the echoes of gunfire, if only spasmodic shooting? And a warwhoop or two, it being common knowledge more redskins than Mexican bandits or renegade whites had been recruited to Corsario's murderous cause?

Rising, patting the black's gleaming neck, he muttered, "Too bad I have to overtire you, boy. But needs must as the Devil — in the form of Corsario — demands."

He remounted. The black snorted as he sank spur, then took off at a gallop, making the miles. He maintained that hectic pace for what seemed a long time and, when next he drew rein, he was plagued by unease. The south lip of the great basin was not far distant now; damn it, less than a half-mile.

From away to the east, he clearly heard the now and again lowing of cattle. There were many ranches east and north of Rowansburg; the community's economy was founded on the cattle business. Colonel Delmer had assumed, and reasonably, that hired hands of the local spreads would arm themselves under orders from the ranchers and force their way through the raiders ringing the basin to reach and help defend the town. He studied the sky. This made no sense. Dawn would break soon.

At sun-up, the black was plodding and panting and the near rim of the basin in sight, but nothing else. He didn't bother to use his binoculars. In the first rays of the sun, the area surrounding the basin was quiet, as quiet as the township down there on its flat floor.

He saw smoke, but it rose lazily from a few chimneys, not from the embers of burnt out buildings. He sensed no tension, saw no activity in Rowansburg's broad main street. Grim-faced, his suspicion chilling his blood, he descended the long slope. Moving downhill was a little easier for the black, but his hooves dragged by the time they reached the basin floor.

Grescoe dismounted and, leading the winded animal by its rein, walked the remaining distance to Rowansburg.

Later, entering the main street, he saw signs of life, a white-aproned man yawning and sweeping the sidewalk outside an early opening cafe, a swamper toting bucket and mop from a saloon entrance, an upper window opening, a woman appearing there to fold her arms on the sill and boredly scan the quiet street.

By the time he reached the sheriff's office fronting the county jail, Grescoe's pulse was racing. He looped his rein over the hitch rail, wondering why the black didn't collapse. Moving up the steps, he pounded on the office door.

It took most of a minute for him to win a response. A muffled voice challenged him from inside.

"Who in blue blazes is that?"

"Lieutenant Grescoe, Eighth Cavalry," he curtly announced. "Now will *you* kindly identify yourself?"

"Damon Kingsmill, county sheriff.

Be right with you."

"Don't keep me waiting, Sheriff! This is a matter of extreme urgency!"

"I don't open up for the president himself before I get my pants on, damn it."

Grescoe waited, fuming, till the door opened. He entered to confront a greying lawman some five feet nine inches tall garbed only in undershirt, pants and boots. From beyond the locked jailhouse door, he heard voices that increased his irritation. Inmates of the Rowan County Jail were rousing from sleep and setting up a clamor of profanity.

Kingsmill moved to the dealwood door, thumped it and bellowed, "Hold it down, you soreheads — or no breakfast!" To his visitor he offered an explanation. "It's kind of rare for me to bunk down in my office but, last night, I just had to. I got Slash Seven and Bar J waddies in there. They got drunk and destructive last night uptown at Marraby's Saloon.

My deputies finally cooled 'em and locked 'em up, but the effort cost 'em — *they* took a beating. We don't have a jailer, so it had to be me minding the office." He gestured to the stove by the filing cabinet. "Coffee oughtn't be cold. Warm maybe, not real hot. Help yourself and tell me what I can do for you."

Grescoe needed the coffee the way he needed to keep on breathing. He filled a tin cup and drained it while the sheriff watched him curiously. Discarding the cup, he put his first question.

"Comancheros, border raiders, Corsario's wolfpack — have they been sighted in this region?"

"It'd be all of nine months since a bunch of Box W hands tangled with a dozen of 'em and sent 'em running," frowned Kingsmill.

"No trouble since then?" challenged Grescoe.

"Nothin," said Kingsmill. "Small party like I told you. Probably needing meat. They'd have run off part of Oley

Wesson's herd but for his boys being so hot for a fight. Want to tell me why you're asking, Lieutenant?"

"Do you have a deputy named Gillis — Sam Gillis?" demanded Grescoe.

"Never heard of any Sam Gillis," said Kingsmill. "My deputies're Chuck Smith and Mitch Holden."

"Describe them," urged Grescoe.

"Well, they're taller than I am . . . " Kingsmill began.

"By how much?" asked Grescoe.

"Both six-footers," said Kingsmill.

"Damn!" breathed Grescoe. "Gillis is your height."

"Now Lieutenant, I'm chief law officer of this territory," Kingsmill pointed out. "Any more questions you have, I'll gladly answer, but it seems to me you ought to satisfy *my* curiosity."

"The regiment is headed this way, responding to a call for urgent help," scowled Grescoe. "The message was delivered by a courier who gave his name as Gillis and called himself a deputy sheriff. He wore a badge — do you understand? He reported that this community was under siege, surrounded by a heavy force of Comancheros led by Corsario himself — hundreds of them."

"Lord almighty!" gasped Kingsmill.

"How else would you expect Colonel Delmer to react?" muttered Grescoe. "He's leading the entire regiment to this basin. Fort Mitchum is virtually undefended, nobody there but women and children and a mere handful of troops."

"So," sighed Kingsmill. "The only thing about this Gillis we know for sure is — he's a convincing liar."

"And one of Corsario's own men, obviously!" snapped Grescoe.

"You aren't saying it, but I'm reading your mind," nodded Kingsmill. "Corsario's after whatever he can loot from the fort, so he's drawn the Eighth north — far from its base. All right, Lieutenant, you have a real emergency so, any way I can help, you only have to ask."

"I winded my mount getting here," said Grescoe.

"Rode ahead of the . . . ?"

"To scout the situation, estimate Corsario's strength, then return to rejoin the regiment and advise Colonel Delmer."

"Yes, that would've been a big help — if we'd been defending Rowansburg from behind barricades. You fit for the ride back? Must be hungry by now."

"I have to leave *immediately*! All I need from this town is . . . !"

"You don't have to say it. Fastest horse we can give you, and I know where to find it. Give me time to throw on some more clothes and I'll . . . "

"Kingsmill — there isn't time!"

"Whatever you say. Let's go."

Kingsmill quit the office with Grescoe. The winded black was led to the town's biggest livery stable. To the lieutenant's relief, the sheriff assured him the proprietor, Rafe Engleman, was an early riser.

Lean and wiry, fresh-shaven, Engleman answered the lawman's summons and lent an attentive ear to his explanation. Kingsmill then declared, "You know which horse it'll have to be, Rafe. Lieutenant Grescoe could commandeer it on behalf of the army, but I'd personally prefer — well — under the circumstances . . . "

"Oh, hell," winced Engleman. "It'll have to be Rio Red." He ran a critical eye over the weary charcoal. "No horse looks its best when out of wind, but I can see this one's a thoroughbred, good shoulders, strong legs. All right, Damon, I'll make the sacrifice. Hate to part with Rio Red but, as you say, under the circumstances." He nodded to Grescoe. "Better make ready to switch your saddle."

As the livery owner hurried into the barn, Kingsmill told Grescoe, "You'll be on the strongest, fastest horse in this part of Texas. Thoroughbred like the black — and Rafe's most prized possession. The Fourth of July races, Red always wins. Not a horse hereabouts can keep up with him. Best we can do for you, Lieutenant."

"Much appreciated," acknowledged Grescoe.

He was hefting his saddle in readiness when, from the barn, Rafe Engleman led one of the finest horses he had ever seen, a smart-stepping, strong-limbed strawberry roan. Engleman helped him ready it for the trail and, while doing so, remarked, "It's unusual I guess, a livery owner offering such advice to a cavalry officer. You mind?"

"If you can say it briefly, Mister Engleman," Grescoe muttered as he secured the cinch.

"He doesn't need much spur," said Engleman. "When you're up out of the basin, give him full rein. Do that, and you'll also give thanks you're an experienced rider."

"It'll be like riding a rocket," warned Kingsmill.

"Gentlemen, I thank you for your

co-operation," said Grescoe.

He swung astride and was at once aware Rafe Engleman was no liar nor prone to exaggeration. The big strawberry roan carried him out of Rowansburg at impressive speed. It seemed only a few minutes passed before he was putting his new mount to the basin's south slope; had he not restrained Rio Red, they would have made the long ascent at a gallop.

Clear of the basin, he gave the animal full rein. This would not be his first fast ride, but he took heart from the feeling it would be his fastest yet.

Misgivings took over now. By stalling the Eighth en route to Rowansburg, he could claim he had gained valuable time for the regiment. But would it be *sufficient* time? He was in no doubt Fort Mitchum was now under attack. Corsario's ruse had succeeded. He would take advantage of a cavalry headquarters manned by a mere handful of troopers. Assault after assault would be ordered. There would be attempts to scale the stockade; so spellbinding a rabble-rouser was Corsario, his motley force would attack as madmen, suicidal, caring nought for their own lives.

Racing southward at high speed, he disciplined himself to think not only of the woman he loved but of all the other women — and the children. How many soldiers left at the fort, how many to man the catwalks?

"Mulligan — a good man, a born fighter," he was thinking. "Two other sergeants if I remember correctly. Yes, Ulric and Elvey will give a good account of themselves. Damn! That's only three! No, more than that. The half-dozen in the guardhouse. They'll have had time to sober up, Yarrow and those other roughnecks. Mulligan would release and arm them the moment the raiding party is sighted. He'll order them to the parapets and, yes, roughnecks they certainly are, but good marksmen. So *maybe* they're holding out.

"Nine soldiers. No, ten, if he included — how in blazes could a man as gentle as Trooper Ainsworth become a soldier? The man was too sensitive. Could *he* be expected to handle his share of the fighting?"

He cleared his mind of these thoughts and concentrated on the area ahead, which the strawberry roan seemed to regard as a challenge, so swiftly did he move. Only once did he force the animal to a halt. It wasn't natural, too much to ask of any animal, he warned himself, that he should maintain such a pace without tiring. Rio Red snorted impatiently, obviously resenting being reined in; but for his disquiet, Grescoe might have found this amusing.

It was not yet 10 a.m. when he sighted the column. He rose in his stirrups and waved urgently. Corporal McBean, who tended to be scornful of military protocol, scorned it now and bellowed to his commanding officer without requesting permission to speak. What the hell? he reflected. He was hollering anyway, rather than speaking.

"Colonel! That ain't the horse I cut out for Lieutenant Grescoe!"

"Column — *halt* . . . !" yelled Major Landis.

The colonel used his field glasses.

"Young Grescoe's riding like a man possessed," he observed.

"I see no Comancheros in pursuit of him, sir," said Landis.

"Can't be any doubt he has good reason for stalling us," opined Captain Harrington. "He always acts responsibly."

A few yards ahead of them, Grescoe brought his mount to a dust-raising halt. Then he offered his report, speaking quickly, but precisely, disciplining himself again; if he were obliged to repeat himself, precious time would be lost.

When Grescoe stopped talking, Delmer's mouth set in a hard line.

His officers traded stunned glances. Only Landis addressed the colonel, and briefly.

"All too clear, sir. Diversionary tactic."

"And such a simple — treacherous ruse," breathed Delmer. "I blame myself. Damn that rogue Gillis! If he's taken alive, I'll *personally* hang him! Major Landis, we're returning to headquarters!"

"Anybody know any short cuts?" Glynn asked as they turned their horses.

"We travelled them to here," growled Surgeon Major Richards. "The fastest way home is to retrace our own trail."

Officers relayed the order to NCOs who rode fast along the column, yelling to the troopers. Horses nickered as their riders quickly wheeled them. The return to Fort Mitchum began with, at Delmer's insistence, his aides falling back to pass the word to the enlistees; this was no time for keeping the regiment in the dark as to the reason they weren't pressing on to Rowansburg.

* * *

Around Fort Mitchum, the temperature had dropped. Though the day was sunny, a cooling breeze swept southward across the flats. Men caught up on much-needed rest, some sleeping, others warily watching the area to which the night raiders had retreated.

Larry and Stretch had repeated their weapons-gathering routine. Ammunition expended was replaced and there was no shortage of pistols and rifles fully loaded; a defender could reach for a firearm fast. To keep the children occupied, Naomi Landis read to them in Barracks 4. With no way of knowing the regiment was even now en route back to the fort, some of the women were apprehensive, but hiding their fears behind a mask of serenity. For this, they won the admiration of the tall trouble-shooters.

Martin Ainsworth had been dozing in a chair. When roused by sounds of movement, his patients were lowering themselves to their cots again. But something had changed. He rose, went to them and frowned at the pistols rammed into their pants-belts. Gleddon glared up at him defiantly.

"All right, kid," he growled. "We're ready and willin', and nothin' you say'll make any difference."

"Rest and eat you said," O'Curran reminded him. "Wait to get our strength back. Well, we had strength enough to take a walk out there and back."

"And arm yourselves," observed Ainsworth.

"If you got any gizzard for a fight, you better do like us," advised O'Curran. "No guessin' how long before the main bunch comes hustlin' home. Still more Comancheros crowdin' us, more of 'em than us."

"They'll get inside the fort sooner or later, you'll see," warned Gleddon.

"And, when they do, it's gonna be every man for himself."

"And for the women and children," said Ainsworth.

"We ain't forgettin' the women and the young'uns," O'Curran assured him.

"Close quarters it'll be," declared Gleddon. "How does that set with you, boy? You ever faced up to an Injun comin' at you with a lance, a knife, a tomahawk?"

"You know I haven't," said Ainsworth.

"Well, by damn, it could happen," Gleddon told him. "*Could* happen? Hell, it's certain."

"I won't enjoy it," Ainsworth confessed. "But, whatever you choose to think of me, you oughtn't assume too much. I'll defend myself if I have to."

"Better do it right," urged Gleddon.

"Else you're a dead soldier — and don't you forget it," muttered O'Curran.

From the entrance to his quarters, Captain Blore pensively scanned the parade ground and the stockades, the men on the catwalks. He was still deep in thought when he caught Mulligan's eye and crooked a finger. The sergeant descended from the east wall and came across to join him.

"Sir?"

"You've been that far north and farther — so have I," said Blore.

"We're talkin' about Rowansburg," guessed Mulligan.

"Yes," said Blore. "It's quiet now, but this is the lull before the storm. Corsario has to launch another assault if he hopes to achieve his purpose before the regiment returns to base."

"That's what Corsario'll be thinkin' about right now," agreed Mulligan.

"So the question in my mind is when," confided Blore. "I've been doing some figuring, Sergeant. We both remember the day and the exact time Colonel Delmer led the Eighth away to begin the advance on Rowansburg. I've estimated their rate of travel and . . . "

"Me too," Mulligan interjected.

"Perhaps we've come to the same

conclusion," said Blore. "We can, for instance, safely assume that the colonel ordered an immediate turnaround, a fast return to base, the moment he realized he'd been duped."

"He'd guess that in less'n a minute, Captain," opined Mulligan. "Wouldn't take him any longer'n that, just one quick look, to savvy all's well up there, nary a Comanchero to be seen. Then he'd make another guess and, like you say, turn the outfit around and head back here licketysplit."

"We may be sure Corsario has considered the time angle," frowned Blore. "I believe we'll sight the regiment by tomorrow's dawn — at the latest. So, if Corsario has made that same calculation . . ."

"Uh huh." Mulligan grunted and winced. "Means tonight's his last chance. But night attacks've been costin' him a lot of men, so more likely he'll come a'raidin' again today."

"What does old Jebediah say about Corsario's strength?" asked Blore. It was an ominous question, but be voiced it calmly. "Does he still believe reinforcements are joining him all the time?"

"He's said it's possible," muttered Mulligan. "Ain't said he'd swear to it, just said it could be."

"I think, in fairness to the men, you should repeat the substance of our discussion," said Blore. "Do it now."

"Sure will," nodded Mulligan.

"The ladies should be alerted," decided Blore. "I'll pay the colonel's wife a visit rightaway."

He was admitted to the parlor of the Delmers' living quarters a few minutes later by Sarah; but for the condition of his leg, he would have made it in one minute, maybe less. Being slowed down by his crutch was a constant irritation, but he looked to his demeanor and greeted the women genially.

They were all present except for Naomi Landis, still keeping the children amused in Barracks 4. Mattie Delmer set her sewing aside and eyed him in polite enquiry. Marj rose, insisted he take her chair, then stood by him with a hand resting on his shoulder. Beth Richards, Elmira Landis, Chloe Toone, Polly Glynn and Leona Harrington sat quiet, waiting. Sarah paced restlessly.

"This is nice, a visit from Captain Blore," smiled the colonel's wife. "You have something to tell us?"

"It has to be said, and there's no easy way, Mrs Delmer," he began apologetically. "I've been calculating the regiment's rate of progress, the length of time it would take to reach Rowansburg — and to return to Fort Mitchum. Sergeant Mulligan concurs with my estimate."

"Captain, I too have given much thought to that question, as you can imagine," said Mattie.

"I've no doubt, ma'am," he nodded.

"I didn't think to consult a map, but of course you'll have done that," she murmured. "The colonel must have reached Rowansburg long before now — am I right?"

"He would now be en route," said Blore. "Leading the regiment south and anticipating Corsario's strategy."

"Please make your point." she invited.

"For heaven's sake, yes!" Sarah showed exasperation.

"Sarah, my dear, patience if you please," chided her mother. "Matters of such importance should be dealt with calmly. And let's not forget the captain is our guest. Proceed, Captain."

"It would please me to be wrong about this," said Blore. "I don't believe we can hope to be relieved before dawn tomorrow. Always assuming the Eighth will stay on the move through the hours of darkness. It's entirely possible there'll be another attack today, any time from now on in fact,"

"And, knowing the territory, Corsario also has considered the time element," Mattie supposed.

"I'm afraid so," said Blore. "But let me emphasize that his calculations must be as rough as mine. There are so many other factors, you see. The colonel may have reached Rowansburg earlier than I've estimated. It's even possible the regiment didn't advance all the way to Rowansburg, in which case they may return to base — well — quite a few hours sooner."

"My father would have no way of discovering he'd been tricked until the regiment reached it's destination," protested Sarah.

"With respect, Miss Sarah, it is possible," insisted Blore.

"How so, Tom?" asked Marj.

"Forward scouts," he explained. "It's a reasonable supposition and standard procedure under certain circumstances. An NCO with three of four troopers assigned to ride ahead and assess the situation. Having done so, they'd hotfoot it back to the main force, and you may be sure the colonel's reaction to their report would be prompt and decisive."

"That's a comforting thought,"

remarked Chloe Toone.

"The not so comforting thought is the prospect of a last desperate attack some time today," frowned Mattie. She nodded to Blore as he rose to leave. "Thank you, Captain. We appreciate your warning. Very kind of you but, more importantly, very practical, far wiser that than keeping us in the dark as to the seriousness of our position."

"We're prepared, I believe," said Leona Harrington.

"So I see," said Blore. Rifles and pistols were very much in evidence on the window ledges, in corners, under tables. "I may rely on you ladies to confine yourselves to this building? If the enemy does succeed in entering the fort, you'll . . . ?"

"We'll fire from the windows," Polly Glynn assured him. "If they mean to seize hostages, we'll not make it easier for them by showing ourselves."

"All they'll see are the weapons we'll be discharging at them," promised Elmira Landis.

Marj Blore saw her husband to the entrance. They paused there a moment, studying each other. She kissed him and he departed while, on the south catwalk, Mulligan parleyed with Jeb Penn and the trouble-shooters.

7

'Let 'Em Hear Us'

THE sergeant stubbed out his cigar and declared, "I've passed it on to the others, everything the captain and me talked of. What it gets down to is today could be their last chance — so we're liable to get busy again real soon. You go along with this, Jeb?"

"Yup, that's how I figure it," nodded the old scout, lowering his spyglass. "No sign of 'em yet, but I reckon it's just a matter of time. And, about reinforcements, you and the cap'n could be right about that too. But we better not forget there's still a horde of the skunks out there — we'll still be outnumbered."

"Well," shrugged Stretch. "Bein' outnumbered ain't the worst could happen to us. Said it before and I'll say it again. We got cover aplenty. They got none."

"And we got guns enough to throw plenty lead their way," said Larry. "We won't lose time reloadin'." He was squatting crosslegged, smoking. "See anything, Jeb?"

"Dust, but that was an hour back," frowned Jeb. "Didn't holler no warnin'. There was just that one big puff, kinda. Wasn't the whole line of dust you see when they come a'chargin' at us."

"One big puff — like a cloud of it?" prodded Larry.

"Uh huh," grunted Jeb. "And, if it was what I fear it was, Mose and Jake better be ready to get blastin' with all them scatterguns their side of the gates."

Larry swore softly.

"They cut a tree down — likely a big'un," he scowled.

"Betcha ass," said Jeb.

"Batterin' ram," Mulligan said grimly. "They plan on forcin' the gates."

growled Mulligan. "I'll make sure Mose and Jake're ready for 'em."

"Take quite a passel of riders to haul it," said Jeb. "Two lines of 'em comin' Injun file, ropes strung under the trunk, cradlin' it, the two lines ridin' level."

"Buckshot at close range'll stop 'em for sure," growled Mulligan. "I'll make sure Mose and Jake're ready for 'em."

"No fire arrows yet," muttered Larry. "But — *this* time . . ."

"Yeah, this time," agreed Stretch.

"They start any fires here, we're in real trouble," fretted Mulligan. "We got Gleddon and O'Curran laid up — makes two less to man the parapets. Can't have the women dousin' fires, can't spare any of us . . ."

"Sometimes I'm fast on my feet," offered Stretch. "I'll give it my best shot, Sarge, try to be in two places at one time."

"No man can do that," argued Mulligan.

"Well," said Larry. "If they come at us with a batterin' ram *and* throw fire arrows, all of us better be ready to do things we never did before."

Jeb chuckled approvingly and observed, "You bucks never give up, do you?"

"None of us can afford to give up, Jeb," declared Larry. "Up till now, we've fought as hard as we knew how, but that was only exercise — compared to what's comin'."

Mulligan grimaced and surveyed the catwalks. Ulric and Elvey were in position to the right of the gates, Janney and Sykes at the west parapet, Frost and Yarrow alone on the north and east catwalks respectively. Then he cocked an ear.

It was starting again, audible away to the south, faint but ominous. The dirge, the death chant.

"Singin' at us again," remarked Stretch.

"Remindin' us they're out there — and they'll be comin' again," said Jeb.

"Damn miserable sound," grouched Larry.

The other defenders had heard it. They were staring south resentfully.

"Mulligan and the captain got to be right, runt," Stretch said quietly. "This'll be the day. They're gonna hit us with everything they got."

"You could make book on it," nodded Larry.

The women and children heard the dirge. So did the three men in the infirmary. Puzzled, Ainsworth asked, "Why do they do that?"

"Injun's ways," Gleddon said in disgust. "And the greasers join in. They learn fast."

"Singin' of how they're gonna massacre every last one of us," muttered O'Curran. "Now we're supposed to spook. Well, damn all them heathens. They ain't spookin' me."

"Oh." Ainsworth nodded understandingly. "Intimidation tactics, an attempt to demoralize us before they attack."

"What's that mean?" demanded Gleddon.

"Pretty much what O'Curran said," offered Ainsworth.

"So why don'tcha say it plain like him?" complained Gleddon.

"Sorry," said Ainsworth.

"Next raid, you forget about tryin' to bar us from gettin' outa here," warned Gleddon.

"Yeah, forget it," growled O'Curran. "I feel a whole lot stronger and so does Red, so we aim to do our share, savvy?"

"You could reach a catwalk," Ainsworth conceded. "Use a rifle too. But, for Gleddon, it would be a foolish move." He eyed the big redhead and appealed for reason. "You can use a revolver, but it would be useless at long range. And climbing steps is something you oughtn't attempt with your ribs plastered."

"If you think we're gonna stay outa this scrap . . . " began Gleddon.

"What if they scale the stockade this time?" challenged Ainsworth. "Suppose some of them get inside? Wouldn't it make better sense for us to pick them off from here? And there's something else. Sergeant Mulligan detailed me to place filled pails at positions close by the barracks and the other buildings, a precaution against their using fire arrows. If an arrow hits a timber wall or a plank roof and ignites it, the fire has to be put out before it can take hold."

"Well . . . " began Gleddon.

"I could do that if it became necessary," Ainsworth decided. "With you two giving me cover from the doorway."

The wounded men gave that some thought.

"Kid's got a point, Red," suggested O'Curran.

"Yeah, well maybe," frowned Gleddon.

From the south, the mournful but threatening dirge continued. Up on the south catwalk left of the gates, the old scout chewed scornfully on the mouthpiece of his corncob. Stretch darted a side-long glance at his partner and read the signs, the gleam in the eyes, the thrust of the square jaw; Larry's blood was boiling, his ire increasing minute by minute.

"Damn caterwaulin'," scowled Mulligan. "It ain't loud. They're a long ways from here and the wind's blowin' from the north, but I can still hear it."

Something snapped in Larry's mind. He wet and raised a forefinger.

"You said . . . " he began.

"From the north," repeated Mulligan. "You heard me. I said the wind's blowin' from the north."

"So the hell with 'em!" growled Larry. "They'll hear us clearer'n we're hearin' them! They like singin'? Let's give 'em some *real* singin'!" He stepped to the inner edge of the catwalk to bellow to the other men, while Stretch grinned and fished out his harmonica. "Hey, you horse soldiers! You had your bellyful of that wailin'?"

"Sure ain't easy on the ears!" came Yarrow's reply.

"Them Injuns and Mexicanos're tone-deaf!" Frost opined from the rear.

And, from the west side, Janney declared, "They can't sing worth a damn!"

"How about we let 'em hear *us*?" urged Larry. "Amigos, if you don't know *this* song, you ought to hang your heads in shame!"

Stretch puffed at his harmonica and, in his powerful, echoing baritone, Larry began the refrain:

"Way down yonder in the land o' cotton

Old times there're not forgotten . . . !"

"Look away — look away . . . " bellowed the grinning Sykes, "look away, Dixieland . . . !"

Moses Elvey and Jake Ulric loudly added their voices:

"In Dixieland where I was born in Early on one frosty mornin' . . . !"

"Look away, look away, look away, Dixieland!" chanted Yarrow and Frost.

Mulligan and Jeb, after wary glances

into the distance, decided the time had come for them to join the performance, and did so.

Mattie Delmer rose from her chair and smiled at her companions.

"Doesn't that gladden your hearts, my dears? And shouldn't *we* be heard?"

"Sopranos and contraltos would be a much-needed improvement," remarked Elmira Landis.

"We can replace the barricades after the performance," said Mattie. "Leona, Polly, clear the doorway. We're going out to the porch."

In Barracks 4, the children had reacted automatically. Boys and girls, even the tiny ones, raised their voices eagerly. Naomi went to the window, took a quick look out, then moved to the door.

"Follow me," she ordered. "Line up on the plank walk, don't move off it. We'll be heard from there. Hurry now."

In the infirmary, Gleddon and O'Curran quit their cots.

"Well," Ainsworth said from the doorway. "We can be sure the Comancheros haven't been sighted — otherwise the ladies wouldn't be out front of the administration building, and Miss Naomi wouldn't be lining the children up out there."

Still singing, suddenly conscious the volume was increasing, Larry peered over his shoulder. The ladies of Fort Mitchum had formed a group and were in good voice; he traded grins with Stretch.

"I wish I was in Dixie — away — away . . . !" trilled the women with pride.

And the children's singing rose high and clear:

"In Dixieland I'll make my stand I'll fight and die for Dixie . . . !"

"Reb song," growled Gleddon.

"What d'you care, pal?" challenged O'Curran. "You're out-numbered by Southerners. I'd as soon be singin' 'The Wearin' O' The Green', but if this's good enough for Mulligan, it's good enough for me — so what're we waitin' for?"

"You know this song, kid?" demanded Gleddon.

"Doesn't everybody?" grinned Ainsworth, and contributed his tenor with his patients joining him.

Another chorus began, the wind carrying the singing of defiant men, valiant women and proud children across the wind-swept plain at such volume that the death chant of the Comancheros was muffled — then silenced.

They didn't need Larry leading them any more. Stretch came to him and, grinning broadly, hooked a long arm about his muscular shoulders. Together, they looked at the smiling, singing women and Naomi and the small fry. She held the smallest child, a little girl, in her arms.

"Ain't this somethin' to see and hear, runt?" the taller drifter said wistfully.

"And to remember," said Larry. "Look at 'em Stretch. This could be their worst day, but they ain't showin' fear. How about them kids? And them women — they're quality."

"Ain't that the truth," agreed Stretch. "Makes a man proud to be Texan, huh?"

"We've always been proud of that, always will be," Larry reminded him.

"I'm just mentionin' it," grinned Stretch.

"They're the best," declared Larry. "Worth protectin' — worth dyin' for."

"We might end up doin' that," opined Stretch.

"We might," nodded Larry. "And, if this is our day to fall, what d'you say we make them sonsabitches do it the hard way, take a lot of 'em with us?"

"I'm with you, ol' buddy," said Stretch. "Just like always."

"Dust south!" yelled Jeb, setting his spyglass aside and taking up a rifle.

Mulligan promptly signalled the women, who began withdrawing while Naomi hustled her charges back into Barracks 4, all of them still singing, bringing the song to its rousing conclusion.

"Away, away, away down south in Dixie

Away, away — away down south — in Dixie . . . !"

Ainsworth spoke quietly to Gleddon and O'Curran.

"You saw the sergeant's signal — another attack."

"We're stayin' right here," said Gleddon.

"To keep our eyes peeled," said O'Curran. "Any of 'em make it over the walls, we better be ready. You too, boy. Time to grab yourself a hogleg."

"Don't worry," said Ainsworth. "I'm ready."

"Kid sounds like he is," Gleddon remarked.

"Damned if he don't," nodded O'Curran.

From the south stockade, the trouble-shooters, Jeb and Sergeants Mulligan, Elvey and Ulric watched the moving dust.

"Fannin' out already," Larry observed as the riders came into view.

"And just like Jeb figured," scowled Mulligan. "Middle bunch haulin' a batterin' ram." He called across to his colleagues. "Mose — Jake — remember now. The shotguns, when they're close enough to feel what you're blastin' 'em with."

"We'll hold 'em back from the gates — they won't get to use that thing," Elvey called back to him. "Rest of you better get set to handle those outriders."

"Looks like they're gonna circle us again," growled Jeb.

"Injuns and Mexicanos," noted Stretch. "And a lot of them Mexicanos used to be vaqueros. They're twirlin' ropes already."

"Set sights for long range!" Mulligan yelled.

Filling the air with war whoops, Indians began their circling movement, the bandidos riding with them — a wide circle.

214

"Leery of our Winchesters," guessed Larry.

The double line of Mexicans hauling the battering ram were advancing faster now, their target the gates. Flanking them, other riders rose in their saddles to rake the south wall with rapid fire, their motive all too clear to the defenders; keep them busy, give their companeros their chance to use the ram.

"No ragged fire, boys!" warned Larry, drawing a bead.

"Let 'em have it!" ordered Mulligan.

Along the south catwalks, Winchesters began barking steadily and, at once, saddles emptied, but the raiders kept coming, their bullets kicking splinters from the top of the stockade, coming too close for comfort.

Mulligan loosed a yelp as a slug shallowly creased his left upper arm, drawing blood. Just that one yelp, a curse or two, and he was doggedly ignoring the smarting of the wound, levering another shell into his breech and taking sight on a redskin loosing an arrow. The arrow sped between Larry and Stretch, dived and fell to the compound. Mulligan squeezed trigger, putting his bullet through the brave's torso and driving him backwards from his pony.

From the east, west and rear parapets, Yarrow, Janney, Sykes and Frost kept their rifles working, scoring on the circling raiders.

"What's your guess, Jeb?" Mulligan demanded over the clamor of gunfire. "When'll they close in to try throwin' them ropes?"

"Likely holdin' back, waitin' for their compadres to bust the gates open," Jeb replied while taking aim. "You readin' their minds, Corsario's mind, friend?"

"Bust in from the front, climb the walls on all sides," nodded Larry. "If he can put a couple dozen of his men inside with us, we're finished — he thinks." He noted the distance separating the bandidos hauling the ram from the gates and yelled advice to Elvey and Ulric. "Gettin' near that time, fellers! Switch from rifles to the scatterguns!"

"Any minute now!" Ulric agreed. To Elvey, he muttered, "Think of how long it must've taken 'em to bring that tree down and hack off its branches. No saws, no axes, just tomahawks and machetes."

"Bottom end's gettin' closer," observed Elvey. "I make it forty yards . . . "

"Too soon," said Ulric.

Moments later, "Thirty yards . . . " said Elvey.

"Twenty-five — twenty — fift — fifteen — *now*!" growled Ulric.

Stretch kept on triggering rifle-fire at the riders advancing behind the battering ram, while Larry tugged the spare Colt from his waistband and cocked it; Jeb and Mulligan quickly switched from long guns to pistols.

The double line of horsemen were urging their mounts to greater speed, the jagged end of the tree aimed at the gates, when Elvey and Ulric rose, dipped the muzzles of double-barrelled shotguns and cut loose. With the loud blasts, Mexicans riddled with buckshot screamed and pitched from their mounts. Elvey and Ulric dropped the discharged weapons, grabbed replacements and did it again, raking the other haulers, while Larry, Jeb and Mulligan picked off as yet unscathed riders with six-gun fire.

The massive battering ram caused a vibration as it thudded to earth, the ropes snaking wildly in all directions like agitated water moccasins. Riderless horses milled in panic, frantic to get clear. Stretch was keeping up a merciless burst with rifles, counting his shots, dropping empty weapons, taking up others, resuming his attack on riders south of the fallen ram.

So much for the attempt to break down the gates. The raiders couldn't hope to ride in close, raise the ram and try again; the quartermaster and farrier sergeants had proved they had ample shotguns and shells aplenty.

Came now the diversion tactic calculated to draw defenders off the catwalks. Flaming arrows were loosed, soaring high, then raining into the compound — those that didn't embed in timber walls or land on plank roofs. Ainsworth at once went to work. Gleddon swore in frustration as O'Curran followed the younger man's example, dashing away from the infirmary entrance to seize a bucket; onehanded, how much water could *he* hope to throw on those fires?

Toting a bucket, Ainsworth bee-lined for the shack in which the residue of coal-oil was stored, a fire arrow stuck in its front wall, the wall beginning to ignite. He got the job done. Half the contents of his pail extinguished that blaze. The side wall of Barracks 2 was burning. He ran to it and the wall hissed as he emptied the bucket on the burning section.

Dropping that pail, he took up another and ran to the sergeants' mess. En route, he detoured to collect a ladder, part of Fort Mitchum's equipment and therefore of stouter construction that those makeshifted by the Comancheros. He set it against the side of the building and climbed quickly to the burning roof. When he emptied the pail, he did it with care, swinging it right and left and tilted so that water fell on every blazing plank.

O'Curran had taken care of fires started by two blazing missiles. Toting another pail, he ran to the administration building. A fire arrow had embedded in the timber lintel of a window. In his haste to extinguish it, he took no time to observe the window was open and barricaded from the inside. He swung, the contents of the bucket doused the arrow and the lintel and two women crouched behind the barricade. They rose, gripping pistols, heads and shoulders saturated, Mesdames Richards and Harrington.

"Hol-eee Mother Murphy . . . !" he gasped.

"No, Trooper, just us," spluttered Beth Richards.

"Beggin' your pardon . . . " he began contritely.

"Not at all," said Leona. "Quite refreshing really. Don't let us interrupt your chores."

Three flaming missiles were checked in flight, then three more. Sykes, Frost and Yarrow left off shooting at circling riders to drop to their knees, raise their rifle muzzles, aim at the airborne arrows and prove their sharpshooting skill.

By mid-afternoon, the defenders were still forcing the raiders to keep their distance. But then, at the worst of all times, the wind dropped and, with no breeze to carry away the dust churned up by pounding hooves, thick clouds of white alkali hovered, obscuring the enemy from view of the men on the catwalks. Mulligan cursed bitterly and, though every defender was on the alert, yelled his warning.

"Watch careful! Don't nobody forget

the bandidos with the ropes!"

Advancing through the dust clouds, Mexicans twirled and threw their reatas.

Loops fell on the points of stockade poles and were pulled tight. From the infirmary entrance, Gleddon sighted four of them adhering to the top of the east wall, roared a warning to Yarrow and drew and cocked a pistol. He quit the doorway, bellowed again, and Yarrow heard him. The first head appearing atop the wall was crushed by the swinging butt of Yarrow's rifle and promptly disappeared.

Gleddon spotted a rising sombrero, braced himself, raised and levelled his revolver, waited for a face to appear under the hatbrim and fired. The face showed an ugly blotch of red in the instant before it disappeared.

Swearing luridly, Yarrow drew a knife and moved along the east catwalk, slashing at nooses, some of which were just about to be pulled tight. He was advancing on another when a Comanche, a fast climber, began swinging over, wielding a tomahawk. Yarrow gave him no time to use it, lumbered at him and swung his blade, slashing the buck's throat. The tomahawk dropped to the catwalk. He grabbed the body by the hair and shoved it back over the wall.

Other loops were dropping over points of the south stockade and, on the north side, Curly Frost was busier than he cared to be, a mite jittery, but resisting panic. Darting a quick glance up and over, he saw no fewer than eight Mexicans and Comanches making a hand over hand ascent. He got his pistol working, slaying two climbers before a bullet burned the right side of his face.

Either Mulligan heard Frost's cry above the uproar or read his mind. He turned to see Frost still shooting, but with left hand clasped to his face.

"North guard needs help," he called to Jeb and the tall men before bounding to the east catwalk.

As he passed Yarrow, that pugnacious scrapper was raising himself to put a bullet in the head of a climber just three feet below. He dashed on, then jerked to a halt and cocked his Colt. One of the redmen came up and over and onto the catwalk directly ahead of him. Teeth bared, eyes dilated, the brave charged him, swinging a tomahawk. He sidestepped, felt the wind of the weapon swishing past his left side, pivoted on the balls of his feet and pressed his six-gun to the naked torso's near side. The Comanche wailed as he squeezed trigger and toppled into the compound.

Reaching the north side, Mulligan cursed and took up a rifle. Frost was grappling with a knife-wielding bandido and two of the same dropping to the catwalk, one hefting a pistol, the other a machete. The Mexican with the pistol was closest. Mulligan made sure of him, dropping to one knee and discharging the rifle just as the pistol boomed.

The pistol dropped and the pistolero followed it, pitching from the catwalk with his arms crossed over his belly. And, by then, the other bandido was at close quarters, slashing with the machete. Mulligan parried with the rifle. The snarling Mexican tried kneeing him in the groin and missed as he back-stepped. Mulligan was in blind fury now and fortunately unaware he was levering the rifle's last shell into its breech. He took a pace backward to avoid another murderous swing of the machete, then threw his weight forward, jabbing the rifle's muzzle into his wouldbe slayer's chest. His trigger-finger jerked, the .44.40 slug bored through the Mexican's heart and on through flesh and sinew as the machete clattered to the catwalk. Mulligan grasped the sagging body and, with a mighty heave, sent it plunging down the outside wall.

He turned to check on Frost. The trooper bled from a knife slash, but his attacker was through using that weapon. It was still gripped in his hand, but he was prone and his head a bloody mess; Frost kept stomping on it with both feet until he heard the sergeant's warning.

"Another comin' over!"

Mouthing profanity, Frost picked up the fallen machete and cleft the skull of a Comanche about to vault the wall.

The old scout was risking his life by leaning over the stockade to discharge six-shooters at climbers who kept coming. Beside him, Larry did likewise, scoring with every shot, till the hammer of his pistol snapped on a spent shell. The point of a lance was thrust almost into his throat. He dodged not a moment too soon, got a grip on the shaft and treated Jeb to an exhibition of brute strength.

When he hauled the lance upward, the brave gripping its other end came with it. Jeb put a bullet in his head and then the lance was Larry's and he was reversing it, taking advantage of his generous height by leaning over the wall and jabbing savagely at the throats of other climbing Comancheros.

Stretch took up another rifle full-loaded and, at the same time, threw a glance over his shoulder and flinched at what he saw. Fire arrows were still hurtling into the fort. One had fallen to the roof of the administration building.

"That's where the women are!" he called to his partner. "We better split up, runt! I got to get over there!"

"'Be seein' you, beanpole!" panted Larry, still wreaking havoc with the lance. "Watch yourself!"

While the taller trouble-shooter made for the nearest steps, one of the troopers manning the west wall stopped fighting abruptly. Biff Janney heard Jerry Sykes' cry of mortal agony, glanced his way and swore. Sykes had been driven backward by the impact of a bullet. For a moment, he teetered on the inside edge of the catwalk, blood welling from his chest. Then he was gone, dropping from sight, dead before he fell to ground.

Roaring like an enraged bull, Janney darted left and right, his pistol roaring at Comancheros coming over the stockade. He couldn't stop them all, couldn't deal with the half-dozen or more dashing to the steps to descend to the compound. Opposite, Yarrow was in a similar plight, but still in action. His gun empty, Janney bent and reached for the weapon nearest to hand, a dropped tomahawk. For some time thereafter, he was even more active, chopping tirelessly at every head rising above the stockade.

On his way to the administration block, Stretch saw the muzzles of guns protruding from its doorway and windows and hastily veered to his right. A timely move. The women opened fire on raiders who'd gained entry and were running across the parade ground, and their shooting wasn't wild.

Though he failed to spot a filled pail, Stretch did what he had set out to do, reached the roof. He found a coil of rope, hastily fashioned a loop, threw it upward and got lucky. It fell about a rock chimney. Thus he was able to scale the side wall and, finishing his ascent, he made straight for the burning section, flopped to his knees, tugged off his already damaged Stetson and pounded at the flames.

When he was through, only smoke was rising, no flames. Then, abruptly, he changed his mind about descending to the compound. What he saw as he gazed around, more and more raiders scaling the stockades, convinced him he could do more good up here than down there. He had managed to bring the loaded rifle up with him and, as well as his holstered .45s, a third six-gun was rammed in his pants-belt. With rock chimney stacks shielding him, he would find targets aplenty before a bullet or a hurled tomahawk found him. He crawled to the stack from which the rope still dangled, got behind it, readied the rifle and began picking off every hostile he could get a bead on.

The din was deafening, the cries of wounded men mingling with the booming of pistols, the barking of rifles, the blast of shotguns. The compound had been invaded, but many who'd scaled the walls were littering it, cut down by hails of lead triggered by the women and well-aimed bullets from the revolvers of the belligerent O'Curran, the keen-eyed Captain Blore and the burly redhead snap-shooting from the infirmary doorway.

Next defender to fall, O'Curran, lurched drunkenly with one bullet left in his sagging pistol and an arrow jutting from his chest. The Comanche bowman responsible was preparing to loose another arrow into him and O'Curran saw him through a red haze of agony, mustered his waning strength, lifted his gunhand, triggered and saw the brave go to ground before he did.

To Martin Ainsworth's horror, the

front wall of Barracks 4, the building sheltering the children, was ablaze. He heard the young ones coughing inside as he toted a filled pail over there as fast as his legs could carry him. The water, hurled at the burning section, did its work. He had quelled the fire, but the effort cost him. Something fiery struck his back and started him staggering forward. As his legs buckled, he dropped his gaze and saw the point of exit; the bullet had torn clear through him and both wounds bled profusely. He groaned as he flopped, then crawled to the wall and turned, bracing his back against it and tugging the Colt from his belt.

His vision was blurring but, as he cocked the weapon, he saw a machete-wielding bandido headed his way, rushing him. He used his cupped left hand to steady the Colt before firing. Suddenly, the Mexican jerked to a halt, swarthy face contorted, mouth agape. Then he stumbled closer, still gripping his machete, and Ainsworth was now too weak to recock the pistol. One more step the wounded Mexican lurched, but now another pistol roared close by, and Blore's aim was true. The bandido crumbled with his head as bloody as his chest.

Turning awkwardly on his crutch, Blore levelled his long-barrelled Colt at a whooping Comanche charging at him with tomahawk raised high. He squeezed trigger and cursed. His pistol was empty. He was drawing his sabre when a bullet knocked his crutch away. Gasping he sprawled on his back. But he had succeeded in drawing his sabre and, as the redskin began his leap, he grasped the hilt in both hands and thrust upward. The brave descended on him, impaling himself, shrieking. The head of the tomahawk dug into earth four inches from Blore's left ear. He rolled clear of the body, withdrew his sabre and began dragging himself back toward his quarters.

From his vantage-point, Stretch had rifle-shot seven invaders. Now he emptied his holsters and triggered at closer targets with his matched .45s, Comancheros on the catwalks.

Riderless horses had fled. The dust was settling when Larry hefted a loaded Winchester, stared away to the south and growled a question to Jeb Penn.

"Have you spotted their chief — Corsario?"

8

The Last Burial Detail

THE old scout reached for another rifle, checked its loading, raised himself and squinted.

"Three sittin' their horses far back there. Where's that blame spyglass of mine? Wait a minute." He focussed on the distant trio. "Well now, one of 'em's Corsario for sure. The fat greaser could be Henriquez. Dunno about the third skonk."

"They ain't all that far back, not if we raise our sights," muttered Larry. "What d'you say, Jeb ol' buddy? We could get ours any time . . . "

"Any time," agreed Jeb. "Helluva lot more of 'em out there."

"So, while we're alive enough to shoot straight, maybe we can discourage these hostiles some," Larry opined with a cold grin. "Maybe they won't feel so warlike if we down the bastard they'd ride through hell for. If our slugs reach all three of 'em, we'll know Corsario's led his last raid."

"C'mon," breathed Jeb. "Let's do it."

They adjusted their sights for long range, ignored the bullets and arrows hurtling past them, aimed and triggered, levered fresh shells into place and fired again, and the faraway trio was suddenly a duo. They maintained rapid fire and saw the other horsemen, moving targets now, jerk in their saddles.

"Make *sure* of the sonsabitches!" scowled Larry.

When their rifles were empty, so were the saddles of the other horses — much to their grim satisfaction. Then Larry grunted, reeled and flopped on his backside.

"How bad?" demanded Jeb, hunkering beside him. "You got much pain?"

"Ain't the pain I got to fret about,"

grouched Larry. He felt at his bloody left leg. "It's the bleedin'. Man leaks too much blood, it'll weaken him. Two holes — so the slug went clear through the calf, didn't hit bone," He squatted a little while longer, just long enough to reload his Colt and holster it and shove a second pistol into his pants. "Won't leave you for more'n a few minutes. There'll be whiskey in the infirmary, or somethin' else to stop the bleedin'. Then I'll get right back to you."

He limped to the nearest steps and, en route, saw Yarrow on the east catwalk, left arm bloody and useless, right hand full of Colt. The trooper was blasting at other would-be invaders, unaware a Comanche buck was on the catwalk, aiming a lance at his back. He was eager to reach the infirmary, but could spare a moment to empty his holster and put a .45 slug through the Comanche's vitals.

While descending, he kept his Colt cocked, quickly scanned the moving figures down below and thought to also raise his eyes to the roof of the administration building. It was a pleasure, his recognizing the pistolero crouched by the chimney with his guns roaring; Stretch was still in business.

He was in pain but suffering no loss of vision when he reached the compound and limped toward the infirmary. The area was strewn with Comancheros who had paid dearly for scaling the walls. Those still in action, five of them, were edging toward the west wall to prevent the women drawing a bead on them from the administration block — and they were not to survive. Larry's Colt roared twice; he scored both times. Blore cut loose with his reloaded pistol from a prone position in the doorway of his quarters and downed another. Also prone, Gleddon fired from the infirmary entrance, his bullet boring into the back of a head. The fifth, a whooping brave, scuttled up the steps to the west catwalk armed with a lance and toma-hawk, and Janney was waiting for him. When the brave's head and shoulders came in swinging distance of the irate trooper's feet, he aimed a powerful kick. The toe of his boot caught the buck under the chin, jerking his head back, driving him off the steps.

Larry watched the redman pitch into the compound, hitting ground head-first, breaking his neck. He recocked his Colt and stared around. The defenders had won a temporary respite. There were still invaders inside the fort, but none of them breathing. He had time, he decided, time enough to take care of his wound and return to the catwalk before the next assault.

Some little distance from the infirmary, he dropped to one knee beside the haggard, pallid Ainsworth. His scalp crawled as Ainsworth spoke weakly, but clearly.

"Nothing you — anybody — can do for me."

"I'll fetch what I need to plug those bullet-holes," Larry said encouragingly.

"Waste of — time . . . " mumbled Ainsworth.

He died with his eyes open. Larry closed them, clenched his teeth, rose and limped on into the infirmary, passing the sprawled redhead.

Gleddon propped himself on his good right elbow and followed the tall man's movements. Larry got it done quickly, rolled up his left pants-leg, yelped and swore; the pain was fiery when he doused both punctures with whiskey, but worth it. At least the wounds were sterile. He smeared ointment, helped himself to a roll of bandage and wound most of it round the aching calf.

Gleddon mumbled at him.

"Got time enough?"

"For what?" Larry demanded.

"To do that again," winced Gleddon. "It happened to me too, Valentine. Same leg, same kinda wound. Damn slug tore clear through."

"Be right with you," said Larry.

The redhead fought back a groan as Larry tugged off his left boot. He treated Gleddon's wound as he had his own. By then, the whiskey bottle was half empty. He took a generous swig, then placed it in Gleddon's eager right hand. Gleddon drained it, tossed it away and made another request.

"Got no feelin' in my left hand. Take it kindly if you'd reload my pistols — ain't partial to the idea of gettin' mine from some Comanchero bastard — with an empty iron in my hand."

Larry obliged.

"Leg feel easier now?" he asked.

"Some," said Gleddon. "I plan on stayin' right here. Good enough position. I can get a clear shot at any more of 'em comin' over the walls. Your buddy still with us?"

"Only reason you don't hear his guns atop where the women are is he's got no targets," muttered Larry. "No shootin' from the catwalks — has to mean they've retreated again. I best go talk to the captain."

The limp was an irritation. It was

typical of him, as he moved along to Blore's quarters, that he assumed his wound would heal fast, a couple of days at most; the Valentine impatience was a permanent condition.

When Larry reached him, Blore rolled over and addressed him urgently.

"It's unthinkable there'd be only one crutch in Major Richard's stores. I'll ask you to fetch another from the infirmary when we're through talking. Valentine — Larry — the hell with formality. Call me Tom and tell me how we're faring. I know we've lost men."

"We got dead and wounded," nodded Larry. "A lot of Comancheros and not many of us, so we couldn't all stay healthy. But, if it makes you feel any easier, Jeb and me figure we downed Corsario — Henriquez too. They were holdin' far back, but a Winchester slug'll travel quite a ways if the sights're fixed right."

"Best news I've heard since the siege began," enthused Blore. "Big reversal for the enemy, Larry. The morale factor, you understand?"

"I savvy what you're sayin', Tom, but us that can still handle a gun ain't through fightin' yet," warned Larry. "What's left of 'em still outnumber us."

"But there's still hope!" grinned Blore. Larry was listening to an officer and a gentleman — and an optimist. "It shouldn't take the regiment much longer to end the journey home. The one thing — the *big* thing — in our favor, my friend. Colonel Delmer never wastes time in a crisis. The moment he realized he'd been tricked, you may be sure he didn't pause to discuss his next move with his staff. Damn it, no! He gave the order for an immediate return to base!"

"Right now," opined Larry, "would be a helluva time for the Eighth to get here." He turned to move out. "Back in a minute. I'll find you another crutch if I have to tear the infirmary apart."

He didn't have to go to such extremes. The spares were easily located, hanging from a rack in a rear corner. He took one back to Blore, then limped across the compound. His partner had descended from his perch, had found a ladder and set it against a wall to permit a faster return to the roof if needs be. Now, having not yet suffered a wound, he was traipsing back and forth to the steps leading up to the stockade, toting dead men. To Larry, he called, cheerfully, "Just tidyin' up, kind of."

"Stay with it, amigo," urged Larry. "Better their dead stay *outside* the fort."

"Just what I'm thinkin'. How's the leg, runt?"

"Be a time before I can kick ass with it."

"Them's the breaks, runt."

"Ain't that the truth."

Somewhat laboriously, Larry climbed to the south catwalk. Jeb Penn's corncob was cold, but jutting from the side of his mouth. He was using his spyglass, studying the activity south. If he was in pain, he wasn't showing it. Larry saw congealed blood at his left upper arm a few inches below the shoulder. Before he could voice his question, the old scout said gruffly, "It don't bleed no more and scarce smarts at all, just a nick."

"How's it look out there?" asked Larry.

"Powwow," said Jeb. "Greasers and Injuns. Still too many of 'em for my likin', but now they got somethin' to wrangle about. We got Corsario and Henriquez sure enough. Big question for them skonks now is who's gonna boss 'em."

Larry glanced across to the other side of the gates and knew a moment of sadness. He hadn't had a chance to get closely acquainted with Farrier Sergeant Jake Ulric, whose body sprawled with legs spread, Elvey hunkered, spreading a bandanna to cover the dead face.

"Damn Comanche made it up here

and put a lance in him," said the quartermaster sergeant. "I shot the bastard." He gestured downward to the almost naked body huddled near the inside of the wall. "I just hope Jake heard me shoot, heard the sonofabitch scream and fall, before he cashed in."

Gazing around, Larry saw Biff Janney reloading weapons on the west side, working briskly, obviously unscathed. Well, miracles sometimes happened. Yarrow was similarly occupied on the east side. The north catwalk was unmanned. He couldn't see Mulligan, just Frost, and prone; he doubted Frost was taking a nap.

Where was Mulligan? He spotted him now, emerging from the infirmary, moving past Gleddon and awkwardly redonning his blouse. The white Larry glimpsed was not Mulligan's bare flesh nor an undershirt; the sergeant had bandaged his own torso. He crossed the parade ground, coming slowly and stiffly, while Stretch was dropping another dead raider over the east wall;

only three more to collect, including the buck who'd slain Ulric.

Joining Larry and Jeb, Mulligan helped himself to a reloaded Winchester.

"Got gashed by a damn lance," he muttered. "Not too deep. Left side. Not deep enough to bust a rib anyway. Fixed me a dressin' for it, ointment and such, bandaged meself good. Be thankful to the Lord and His Holy Mother the surgeon major left plenty of everything in the infirmary." His face clouded over. "Young Ainsworth would've patched me better and faster."

"Kid cashed in just as I reached him" Larry said grimly. "Knew he was a goner, didn't whine none before he went."

"Frost never knew what hit him," scowled Mulligan. "Wild slug got him right 'tween the eyes." He glanced to his right. "Aw, hell. Jake."

"Regiment oughta be proud of them that's died," said Jeb.

"Damn right," agreed Mulligan.

"Wasn't a boyo gave his life cheap. Kept fightin' till they dropped — may the Lord take their souls."

"How d'you rate our chances now, Emmett?" Elvey called to him.

"I calculate we got only a couple hours of daylight left," replied Mulligan. "If they wait till dark, it'll go bad for us, specially if there's no moon. If they charge any time now and circle us, we got big trouble. If we can stop 'em circlin' us, we might still hold 'em off till Gabriel blows his horn."

"Till what?" frowned Larry.

"Gillespie, the bugler," explained Mulligan. "His given name happens to be Gabriel. Mighty fittin'."

"They ever gonna make up their minds, Jeb?" growled Larry.

"We'll know soon enough," said Jeb.

Minutes later, they heard the war whoops. The Comanche yells echoed across the flats and were heard by Mattie Delmer and her companions and Naomi, still in Barracks 4 with the children.

"They're yippin' again," winced a small boy.

"Don't worry about that sound, Linus," soothed Naomi. "They believe it proves they've braver than the soldiers, but they're wrong."

Jeb set his spyglass aside and announced, "They're chargin' — comin' bunched — 'case you jaspers ain't noticed."

"Beanpole!" yelled Larry.

"Yo!" came Stretch's answer.

"Up here with us!" urged Larry.

"Janney — Yarrow . . . !" bawled Mulligan.

"On our way, Irish!" yelled Janney, and he and Yarrow advanced along their catwalks, both hefting armloads of rifles.

"Take up your positions with Sergeant Elvey," ordered Mulligan. "Adjust your sights. We ain't waitin' for 'em to get close. Choose targets — and fire when ready!"

The seven riflemen positioned along the south stockade aimed for riders leading the charge, opened fire with deadly accuracy and caused chaos. As the leaders fell, some of the horses stumbled. Oncoming riders stumbled over them and were thrown. The defenders, mainly Larry and Stretch, dropped six before they could remount, and then the raiders were retreating.

"That shook 'em some — kind of broke the monotony too," drawled Stretch. "But now . . . "

"Now they'll rally and come at us again," growled Larry.

"They'll *keep* comin'!" raged Elvey.

"Let 'em!" snarled Yarrow. "And we'll have us a turkey shoot!"

The next charge began twenty minutes later. As he cut loose with a Winchester, Larry reflected the original strategy, Corsario's treacherous plan, was being adhered to; the Comancheros were still hell-bent on defeating Fort Mitchum's defenders and taking female hostages.

Flanking Larry, Stretch and Jeb kept up a murderous burst of rapid fire. Mulligan had edged closer to the gates and his weapon was as busy as theirs and Elvey, Yarrow and Janney were making every shot count and forcing another retreat, but at risk to life and limb. Enemy bullets, arrows and lances embedded atop the stockade or hurtled over; death was dangerously close to the defenders, but they weren't budging.

"Hell's bells!" shouted Elvey. "They backed up — but only fifty yards!"

"Now there're comin' at us again!" scowled Jeb.

In later years, men of the Eighth Cavalry would recall this final assault as a suicide charge. Comanches and Mexicans advanced at full gallop, rising in their saddles with rifles chattering.

Janney loosed a wail and lurched backward with his right shoulder bloody, would have toppled from the catwalk had Yarrow not grabbed at him and shoved him to his knees.

"Stay down, Biff," he advised.

"I ain't quittin', damn it!" gasped Janney, fumbling left-handed to tug a pistol from his belt.

"They ain't close enough for you to score with a handgun," retorted Yarrow. "Stay down!"

Stretch dropped an empty rifle, rearmed himself and growled to his partner, "They take a lot of discouragin'." To his disquiet, Larry was grinning. "Runt, you okay?"

"Never felt better," Larry said with relish. "Anybody else hear it?"

"*I'm* hearin' it!" cried Mulligan.

"By dawg," chuckled Jeb. "Gabriel done blew his horn!"

They all heard it now, not only the defenders, but the attack force, Gabriel Gillespie sounding the charge. Gazing north, they saw the Eighth advancing, two hard-riding bands of horse soldiers, one large party charging the Comancheros with rifles barking, the other party circling to block the retreat of the suddenly scattering hostiles.

The defenders at last relaxed, lowering their weapons, leaning against the stockade to build and light smokes. Yarrow helped Janney to his feet so that he too could view the spectacle. Predictably, redskin allies of the dead Corsario died fighting, screaming defiance. Just as predictably, the bandidos dropped their weapons, raised their hands and babbled in their native tongue.

"Ain't got the gizzards of them that took the Alamo, runt," Stretch said contemptuously.

"Well," said Larry. "Santa Anna wasn't surrounded by Texas Cavalry."

Soon, the men on the south catwalk knew it was over, really over, the siege of Fort Mitchum. In the waning light of late afternoon, they saw troopers circling Mexicans squatting bunched. Of the Comanches, there were no survivors. Colonel Delmer and three officers, Majors Richards and Landis and Lieutenant Grescoe, were approaching the gates followed by Corporal McBean and a dozen troopers.

Mulligan called the order to open the gates, then wondered aloud, "Have we got two men strong enough to do that?"

"Hey, amigo!" Stretch waved to Yarrow. "You and me, okay?"

While the gates were being opened, the other men descended from the south catwalk, and not as agilely as had Stretch and Yarrow. Jeb, Mulligan, Elvey and Larry were weary. Janney somehow managed to get down unaided. Then the colonel's party was entering and Mulligan and Elvey saluting him.

Delmer returned their salute and gazed about anxiously.

"Quit your frettin', Colonel suh," grinned Jeb. "Women and young'uns're safe."

"Thunderation!" exclaimed Delmer. "Jeb Penn — bloody but as salty as ever!"

"Too old to be an army scout no more you said," jibed Jeb. "Well, by dawg, not so old I didn't spot Corsario's raiders way southeast of here."

"He hightailed it for the fort to warn you," said Larry. "But you weren't here."

"And who might this civilian be?" demanded Landis.

"Might be a traveller name of Larry Valentine, friend," drawled Larry. "Matter of fact, I'm damn sure I am, and just as sure that stringbean patting your horse's butt's my ol' compadre Emerson, called Stretch."

"Like to get this said right off, Colonel," said Mulligan. "Wasn't for Jeb and these fiddlefoots — who happen to be of decent Irish blood — we never could've held out."

"Gentlemen, the Eighth Cavalry regiment is deeply indebted to you," acknowledged Delmer.

"Yup, you sure as hell are," agreed Stretch.

"But think nothin' of it," shrugged Larry.

"Casualties?" asked Landis.

"Sergeant Ulric and Troopers

O'Curran, Sykes, Ainsworth and Frost died defendin' the fort," reported Mulligan.

"Dear God," sighed the colonel.

"Wounded?" frowned Major Richards.

"Well, sir, there's only a couple of us won't need medical attention," said Mulligan. "Trooper Yarrow and our good buddy Emerson."

"Corporal McBean, you and a half-dozen troopers will assist the wounded to the infirmary," said Richards. "I'll attend them at once, starting with the critical cases."

The women and children had emerged. Accompanied by his wife, Captain Blore presented himself to his commanding officer. As Delmer dismounted, he began an apology, "I should've been at the gates to tender my report, sir, but . . . "

"Sergeant Mulligan and old Jeb told me enough, Captain," said Delmer. "And my eyesight isn't failing, so I'm well aware the Comancheros laid siege to my headquarters. Also, Captain, I need no assurance that you maintained command here with Sergeant Mulligan as your aide."

"Had it not been for this damned leg . . . " began Blore.

"Now, Tom," soothed Marj.

"Mrs Blore, it would be futile for your gallant husband to claim he avoided action," Delmer said with mock severity. "The flap of his holster is unfastened and . . . " He looked at Blore again. "Captain, clean your sabre when you can find time. I see blood on it."

"Begging the colonel's pardon, may I enquire how you managed to return to base earlier than I anticipated?" asked Blore.

"We have Lieutenant Grescoe to thank," Delmer told him. "Some distance south of the basin, he volunteered to make a forward scout. So the regiment had advance warning that no Comancheros were besieging Rowansburg. That, of course, could only mean Corsario had drawn us away by a ruse and was attacking the fort. I can but hope Gillis, who the Rowansburg sheriff had never heard of, has been taken alive."

"Sorry, Colonel," said Blore. "You'll be denied the pleasure of hanging that renegade. Larry and Jeb killed Corsario, Henriquez and a third man with long-range rifle fire. I'm sure we'll find the third man was Gillis."

A short time later, though the infirmary was crowded, Stretch ambled in to rejoin his partner and Mulligan, who had insisted they be last to have their wounds examined by Major Richards.

"You're lookin' kind of smug," Larry observed. "But that's fine by me. You got a right, and I'm still wonderin' how you got out of this ruckus without a scratch."

"That ain't what I'm happy about," confided Stretch.

"Somethin' else?" prodded Larry.

"Uh huh," grinned Stretch. "Big burial detail out there, all the

Comancheros we downed. There's moonlight and plenty lamps to see by, so the soldiers got them Mexicans workin' their butts off diggin' holes. Near forty of them bandidos got captured. I figure they'll get the job done by sun-up, the flats'll look a whole lot cleaner then — and all forty of 'em'll be bone-weary, beat right down to their fancy boots."

"They'll be turned over to the rurales," predicted Mulligan. "Tried and hung in their own country — and good riddance to bad cess."

"Want to hear somethin' else?" offered Stretch.

"We got nothin' to do but listen," yawned Larry.

"That ornery redhead — Gleddon?" said Stretch. "Right outside this place I see sassy Sarah kissin' her purty lieutenant. And there's that ornery redhead . . . "

"Gleddon," said Mulligan.

" . . . floppin' by the door," nodded Stretch. "And damned if he didn't holler at her. 'Miss Sarah,' he says. 'That Ainsworth boy died brave. I figured you ought to know.' And she kind of spooked and started shakin' and the lieutenant took her away."

"She always was wrong about young Ainsworth," muttered Mulligan.

★ ★ ★

Mid-morning of the morrow, when the fallen heroes of the siege were laid to rest with full military honors in the Fort Mitchum cemetery, the flats surrounding the stockade were clear of the raiders' dead. No mounds. Comancheros had been buried deep and the ground smoothed over by prisoners exhausted and demoralized by their all-night labor.

Some five days later, with Larry's wound having responded to Major Richards's treatment, the drifters were ready to leave. They were at first conducted to the Delmer parlor where the colonel, his wife and the other women wished them Godspeed and warmly thanked them.

"I am assured by Captain Blore and Sergeants Mulligan and Elvey that your energy, your wit and your fighting spirit helped swing the odds in Fort Mitchum's favor," declared the colonel. "You gentlemen and, of course, the indomitable Jeb Penn. Many years have passed since you wore the uniform of the Texas Cavalry, but there's no doubt in my mind you are still cavalrymen at heart."

"You could be right about that, Colonel," said Larry. He nodded to the smiling women. "Our respects, ladies."

The quartermaster had forced ample provisions on the drifters. Their horses were saddled and all gear secured. Before mounting, they said their goodbyes to Mulligan and Red Gleddon, the latter informing Larry, "I done changed my mind, Valentine."

"Don't want to fight me?" grinned Larry.

"What the hell?" shrugged Gleddon.

"We fought a whole pack of Comancheros, so we were comrades in arms." He winked as he added, "Besides, you're leavin' now and I got a busted arm ain't healed yet."

"Ride safe, boys," urged Mulligan.

They mounted and started for the gates, trading grins as the small fry of Fort Mitchum sang 'Dixie' to them. One last farewell before they rode out; old Jeb confronted them to wish them well.

"Stayin' on, Jeb?" asked Stretch. "Colonel decided the Eighth still needs you?"

"Damn right," declared Jeb. "It ain't that I'm young, but it's for sure I'm too spry, too blame useful, to be pastured out."

Leaving Fort Mitchum behind them, pushing northward, Larry sadly remarked, "Old places won't look the same. I ain't sure we ought to stay headed north."

"I'm gettin' the same feelin'," said Stretch.

"You're some homely hombre,"

frowned Larry, appraising him sidelong. "But I swear you look uglier with nothin' on top of your doggone head. What happened to your hat?"

"It quit on me," said Stretch. "Wasn't just the bullet that tore it right off my head. I used it to slap out a fire and, by the time I did that, it looked plumb toilworn."

"We'll swing west," Larry decided. "Travel into New Mexico Territory and, first town we find, we buy you a new tile."

The trouble-shooters pointed their mounts westward to ride away from their homestate and from memories of another battle, another crisis that might have cost them their lives. They had survived to fight again.

And would.